Trusted Friends and Lovers

Selected Short Stories

Burkey & Breakfield

Published by

ICABOD Press

ISBN paperback: 978-1-946858-73-3
ISBN hardback: 978-1-946858-75-7
ISBN eBook: 978-1-946858-72-6
ISBN audiobook: 978-1-946858-74-0
Library of Congress Control Number: 2024902246

Cover, interior and eBook design:
F + P Graphic Design, FPGD.com

Created in the USA
Women's Contemporary | Romance

To Trish
Burkey and Breakfield

Contents

Dear Readers,

Welcome to our first edition of selected short stories.

The seven stories we included hold a special place in our hearts, and now we hope in yours. We are beyond thrilled to show you a different side of our storytelling. These particular characters told us they wanted to share the pivotable points in their lives where sparks flew, and decisions rocked their world.

If this is your introduction to the Enigma Series universe, we hope you will consider exploring our other books. You can find these in bookstores worldwide or visit *EnigmaSeries.com* for samples.

Happy reading,

Rox and Charles

P.S. We look forward to your review. *Thank you.*

Fears, Tears, or Cheers

*L*ily beamed with delight at the growing crowd gathered in Flower's dining room at her Texas bed and breakfast. The late morning sun filtered through the blooming plants outdoors, highlighting the purples, whites, and rose colors currently in season. Rushing from one table to another, it was no surprise that Jo and JJ were the gossip de jour in this little community. During their vacation, they solved a massive problem, and now the town considers them family. Oblivious to the conversational din, the couple appeared focused on one another. Lily noted Jo crossed her legs, bumped JJ, then raised her eyebrows and giggled. Lily would keep their confidence, caring for them like her children.

Lily listened to the talk from her patrons at Jo and JJ's breakfast party on the warm, enclosed patio cooled by the rotating ceiling fans. She served mimosas, freshly baked pastries, hot sausage patties, and omelet concoctions that filled the air with mouthwatering scents. The tables included thirty or so new friends. Everyone voiced their opinions of the heroic exploits of the young couple with the embellishments growing, typical of small-town chatter.

"Y'all are famous, ya know?" she conspiratorially whispered, leaning into Jo. "And I don't mean anyone here knowing the infamous world-class model, JoW, with her abundant dark hair and girl-next-door smile from Brazil. Or her heart-throbbing protector sitting next to her, with his thick wavy hair, mesmerizing coffee-colored eyes, and killer smile always." She smirked. "And I won't share if I can get an autograph later."

Standing tall, Lily loudly cleared her throat and announced, "That highfaluting computer stuff you pulled together to trap those horrible criminals was lifesaving. Everyone owes you a debt of gratitude. I think the mayor is presenting you with the key to the city before you leave. We knew something was going on, but you sweeties nailed it. The townsfolk probably need to erect statues of you both!"

Lily noted with a grin that her gushing tribute didn't register with the two young lovers who stared contentedly into each other's dark eyes. Their wistful smiles and longing stares sheltered them from the uproar. "I bet they're looking for their elusive future," she muttered as she picked up plates at nearby tables and watched them pick at the array of delectable items on their plates. Lily clucked and fussed around them like a mom, hoping her chicks were happy. Now and again, someone stopped and slapped JJ on the back with a word of thanks. One of them offered a polite comment that kept Lily's endless conversation running, accentuating her southern twang. Lily rushed to the kitchen to add food to the sideboard.

JJ noticed the conversation dissipated after the plates were cleared and the coffee cups refilled. In the ensuing calm, he said, "Jo, this has been a great week, even if more exciting than planned. Thanks for making it so special. I'm sorry we're out of time, with no resolution on our future."

Jo ruefully smiled, her eyes twinkling. "I need to meet the other models on location by tomorrow evening. Your Aunt Lara is wonderful, and I'm glad she owns Destiny Fashions of Brazil. She's the perfect adopted mom for me but a tyrant on meeting work schedules."

"I'd like to tag along to the shoot and lend a hand." JJ waggled his eyes and inclined his head in all seriousness. He took a breath, feeling anxious. "Unless this is the moment," he whispered, "when you suggest another space break until the holiday event at Uncle Carlos and Aunt Lara's."

JJ saw a shadow cross her face as she frowned.

"I'm not certain where we fit together as a couple. You're a brilliant geek. I'm just a Brazilian model working for your aunt's company. I see how much you thrive within your computer detective world. I'm not a part of that space." She reached one hand to cover his. "Working with you in this town on our vacation has been fun and exciting. You're extraordinary in your element. However, I feel like we're on again, off again. I'm scared we'll fail. Work calls each of us, and our careers are as different as cake from ice cream."

JJ grinned as he added, "And whipped cream."

The rise in the corners of her lips verified that she knew it was one of his favorite toppings on nearly anything. He searched her eyes, hoping to make her understand. "What do you want? I can work from anywhere. Aunt Lara and Uncle Carlos are attending this last shoot of the year. I don't think they'd mind if I joined. I can work remotely; I want to be near you as we head for the holidays."

JJ leaned forward, stroking the top of her hand with his fingers. He loved feeling her soft skin. "I'm looking forward to the annual festivities as long as you're there. I think Gracie and Jeff are going. You'll like my sister."

He watched as she moved ideas around in her pretty head. They'd discussed her concerns about fitting into the family she thought too successful for her. Yet, she was a superstar model recognized by millions.

"JJ, I'll remember this town as one with a big heart. I like the calm and people who I see as friends we made together. Time with you is like coming home."

Jo's face showed her concerns, like someone on a high dive, afraid just to jump. Her mouth opened slightly as if to speak when Lily burst onto the scene again, bringing more gossip to share.

JJ and Jo said their goodbyes after breakfast, promising Lily to keep in touch. They drove to Austin Airport and dropped the rental car in time to meet JJ's parents' arrival in one of Destiny Fashions' private planes. His father was the pilot for the models. The Gulfstream jet roared up to the designated boarding ramp of the regional airport. JJ shook his head, hearing the engines whine, powering down. The gangway lowered, and the pilot and co-pilot, JJ's parents, Juan and Julie, deplaned. JJ knew Jo enjoyed them. His father, the reflection of how he'd look when he grew older, offered a contagious smile across his swarthy-complexioned face, his toned muscles rippling under his shirt. His mother, fair-haired and still lovely, moved with the grace of a ballerina.

JJ chided, "Why the bigger G600 for this trip? The G500 has the range to get us to the location and is more economical. Or is this a bus ride where you stop and pick up others to fill this jet-powered barn?"

Juan winked at Julie and snidely commented over his raised hand. "Is this where you, hand over heart, swear you're not bossy, only certain of what everyone should be doing, son?"

JJ lowered his head slightly, hiding a grin. "Yes, Father, forgive me, for I have sinned. Since you promoted me to run the business, I've evolved into Chief Master Sergeant Juan Jr. Truthfully, issuing orders to get things done feels right. But pulling that card on my parents is reprehensible, especially with Christmas coming."

Laughter ensued, followed by hugs and handshakes. Jo and JJ retrieved their bags to load them into the cabin area.

Juan collared JJ. "Come help me with the ground check while the techs refuel. I bet you still remember how."

JJ struggled to hide his annoyance. "Yes, of course. Now we're looking for missing wings or wheels? And you want me to ensure the tail is still in the right place?"

Juan clucked his tongue and shoulder-bumped his son. "I remember what that probation officer asked me before discharging you to my custody. *Are you sure?*"

"I should know better than trying to match your rapier-like wit, Dad." He chuckled. "Thanks for taking us to the Christmas shoot and pre-Christmas event."

"Oh, good. She liked your idea to stick close. Things might get serious."

JJ hugged Juan, grateful to spend time together and knowing his dad enjoyed their banter.

While JJ and Juan were doing the ground check, Julie loaded luggage with Jo. She looked around, making sure everything was secured. She looped an arm around Jo's waist, and they moved toward the sitting area to wait for the boys to finish.

"You look rested. I hope the week together helped you two figure things out. You know how much I adore you. You're like a daughter." Julie cleared her throat. "I don't want to pry, but are you back together?"

Jo looked at her with an expression of doubt and hope. Again, Julie thought this girl couldn't hide anything; her face showed her feelings. Because of this, her photos were wildly convincing and sold so many Destiny Fashions.

"Julie, the week was fantastic, what with the detective work and sleuthing. We laughed, talked, and worked together while plotting and behaving like kids on a treasure hunt. It amazes me how well we fit." Jo giggled a bit and blushed. "Then I think about his abilities, and I worry. Here we are on our last vacation day, right where we started. We both questioned our long-range plans. I'm afraid of not being smart enough to be in his world, and he's scared of holding me back from modeling success. They say opposites attract, but when two people are so different, can it ever work?"

Feeling sad, Julie thought about how best to convey her thoughts. She schooled her features into a neutral expression. "Perhaps if you both stop analyzing each piece and concentrate on learning if you want to be a couple, it'd be easier. Find your common ground and build from there. After all, it worked for Juan and me. I assure you, we're as opposite as sugar and vinegar. And, I'm the sweet part."

Juan and JJ finished the preflight routine, then moved up the gangway into the cabin. JJ grinned. "The fuel tanks are topped up. We're ready to request tower clearance for takeoff, Captain." He saluted, did an about-face, and hurried to slip into the seat next to Jo. He leaned in for a quick kiss.

"Why do you look like the cat that swallowed the mouse?" Jo asked.

JJ chuckled, "Dad regaled me with some humorous stunts he pulled on one of his first students. One story struck me. He said he was in a single-engine, high-wing prop plane with the engine idling. A young guy jumps in and says, *Let's go.* Dad takes off and circles the airport, staying clear of the traffic pattern. After a few minutes, the guy says, *Well, that's enough. Go ahead and land.* Not missing a beat, Dad responded, *I haven't learned that lesson yet.* The student panicked and demanded, *Aren't you the pilot?* My dad does his sheepishly little-boy routine and says, *no, I thought you were.* The guy turned all shades of green until they touched down smoothly on Mother Earth."

They howled at the visual hilarity.

Juan stated, "All right. Get situated and strapped in, except for you, JJ. I need you to lean over my shoulder to read the gauges as we take off. You'll do it on our landing, too. I forgot my glasses, so you might do it several times during the flight to be safe."

Juan's face didn't flinch as he kept eye contact. JJ felt the alarm crawling up his spine but met his dad's eyes, sensing he was being played.

JJ let out the breath he held when his dad delivered his boyish grin.

"Made you look."

"You had me for a moment, Dad."

"True, but you didn't show it."

Jo laughed as Julie interrupted the banter. "Juan, this is a long flight with a stop tonight in Lima. Let's get going so we can get a good night's rest. Jo needs to be in front of the camera the day after tomorrow."

Juan saluted his wife and turned toward the cockpit while JJ quietly slid into a seat by Jo and whispered. "Aunt Lara is a stickler when it comes to you."

"It's part of why I love her being my adopted mom. Julie," asked Jo, "how long is the flight to Lima?"

"It's a little over seven hours. I secured us rooms at a hotel not too far from the airport. We've stayed there before; the beds are like sleeping on a cloud. We'll be up early the next morning for a fast five-hour leg to Rio. I promised Lara you'd be well rested. You can snooze on the five-hour trip to our destination."

"Perfect, I love flying and always feel rested. Thank you both."
Jo tugged the pillow from beside her seat and tucked it under
her head.

JJ reached over to hold her hand. "If you need anything, let
me know."

She grinned. "Flying private is a lot more comfortable than
commercial. You can pick the music or the movie."

Jo watched as Julie went to help Juan as the co-pilot. Juan often
flew the models, and Julie enjoyed sitting in the right seat.

Jo slept most of the Lima to Rio flight and felt rested, even
with butterflies of excitement twirling in her stomach. She
moved to the window, delighted to survey the location for
the fashion shoot from the air. "JJ, I can't wait to see the gang.
Look at the Rio shoreline and the luscious greenery."

She felt his body press against hers as he leaned to look below.

"It's certainly greener than Texas. More water, too. You're
going to have so much fun. How does it feel to photograph
spring and summer clothes at the cusp of winter?"

She laughed. "I think it'll be warm."

When they landed, the Destiny Fashions' driver met the
plane at Rio de Janeiro airport.

Jo liked and admired Julie as she took charge.

"Dwayne will take you to the resort Lara commandeered for the fashion shoot. It has lovely places near the water along with some rainforest access. I don't think you've been here before, Jo, but you'll love it. Juan and I have some business to attend to, but we'll see you later."

After everyone hugged, Julie leaned into JJ and gave him a sly smile. "We brought the larger G600 to take everyone back to São Paulo for the holidays at the Bernardes Estate after the photos are done. Jo, Lara is thrilled to feature you for the new season of Destiny Fashions. JJ, behave yourself, or your aunt will box your ears.

JJ chuckled. "Always, Mom! See you soon."

Dwayne opened the limousine's back door. "Nice to see you, Miss Jo. You, too, JJ."

They slipped onto the backseat and settled as Dwayne walked around the vehicle to drive. He looked at the rear mirror as he spoke. "Lara said if you felt good, I should take you directly to the shoot."

"Dwayne, that's sweet of you to worry. I'm good and ready to see everyone and the clothes."

Dwayne released a sigh of relief. "Good. I'll deposit your bags with the concierge to deliver them to your rooms. The hotel is reserved for Destiny Fashions' crew for the week."

"Thank you," Jo said. "I bet you're glad you get to join the crew in this beautiful place."

"I sure am. It gets a little humid in the late afternoon, so Miss Lara likes to start early."

"I'm glad we left just before dawn this morning. It's a beautiful day."

Jo grinned and clasped JJ's hand as they made the short trip to the staging area. One tent for changing and makeup, plus a large canopy provided shade with chairs and a table. Lush green plants were along the edges, highlighted by the brilliant blue sky dotted with puffy clouds.

When the limousine stopped, JJ got out and extended a hand to help her from the car. She quickly kissed him. "I'll see you later, honey," and rushed toward the models, exchanging greetings.

Jo turned, saw Lara, and walked toward her. Jo felt Lara's eyes sweeping across her body from top to bottom.

"Glad you made it, sweetie," Lara added a hug. "As your mom, I missed you. As your employer, it doesn't look like you gained an ounce, so no alterations. Hurry, get inside the models' tent for makeup, and check out the outfits on your rack. They're numbered. If the light is right, we'll do the first four or five on the line. I have a few details to work out here before we start."

"Thanks. I'm on it."

Jo admired how Lara, a successful business owner, managed all the details. Each time they worked together, Jo learned something new and gained confidence. She turned to see JJ finding a spot to watch under the canopy.

Jo wiggled her fingers in a silent farewell, turned with grace, striding confidently to the designated area.

Only the makeup artist and seamstress were inside. Spotting her name, Jo rushed to the rack, running her fingers over the soft, colorful fabrics, sighing at the textures while imagining how they would feel against her skin. "Today will be a blast. Help me dress, Mary, please. Then you can do your magic, Jane. I washed my hair this morning, so it should work."

Mary grabbed the first outfit while Jo shimmied out of her clothes. They worked together to arrange the folds of the outfit, which settled perfectly over her slim figure. "No changes needed. It fits like a glove. Pretty."

Jo walked over to the mirror, turning this way and that. "Thank you, Mary. Your work is flawless."

Mary draped a lightweight cape over Jo. Jane used a stool with her makeup pallet on a stand for easy access. Jo stood still as Jane brushed her brows and highlighted her eyes with eyeliner and mascara. "Jo, you have the longest lashes of all the girls. I am adding a little lavender to your lids for this outfit. As your outfits change, I can darken the shades to compliment the colors of each fabric." She crimped Jo's lashes and looked her over with a critical eye.

Getting off the stool, she chuckled. "I think you spent some time in the sand; you've got a glow. Turn." She began brushing Jo's long hair. "I think with this outfit, we can leave your hair down. The wind may pick it up, but Lara thought the silky cloth would move in the same direction. If it doesn't work, I can make a quick change. Turn." She picked up a couple of colors and leaned them against Jo's skin and the fabric. "This lip cover is a little lighter, and we can increase colors as you change. Does that work for you?"

"Absolutely. It's a barely-there color, but it looks like it has sparkles."

"Exactly, hold still." Jane shaded Jo's lips with a brush to ensure the color was even. "Perfect."

Jo turned to the mirror and nodded. "Thanks, you two." She left the tent, overhearing the discussion between Lara and JJ.

"Aunt Lara, I'm not sure why I even doubted you." He snickered after looking at his watch. "Fifteen minutes on the dot. And she looks even more beautiful."

Jo playfully swatted his arm.

"Enough, we need to catch the light. JJ, you're distracting my top model. Go." She waved JJ toward the adjacent rest area with umbrellas, chairs, and tables, then strode toward the crew.

Jo headed toward the rest of the models under the canopy to wait her turn.

Lara conferred with Miguel, her head photographer. They'd worked together from the very beginning of Destiny Fashions.

"Are we ready?"

"The alternate cameras are set to get candid shots like you asked. They're on timers." He looked at Lara and then back on the ground several times."

"Are you all right or just trying to avoid telling me we have no film? Spit it out, or my imagination will run wild," she grinned.

Miguel swallowed. "What if we try doing aerial photos using the newest toy in my camera bag, my battery-operated drone? This quadcopter drone carries a remotely controlled video camera capable of zoom shots. We'll still do standard stills, but this might add a fun perspective and dimension to some of the videos you wanted. Maybe a differentiator."

Lara tilted her head, considering the possibilities, then agreed. "Miguel, that's a great idea." She called to the models. "Ladies, go toward the beach area we scoped this morning. I had the guys set up another pop-up with water bottles on a table. Show Jo her starting point, please. She's up first." Lara refocused on the crew. All right, folks, let's make certain the drone has enough open air to allow Miguel to concentrate on positioning the eye of the camera, not navigating obstacles. How about you start thinking of a name for it, too? If this does what Miguel hopes, we must give it a byline."

Lara was pleased when she located her seat to direct when necessary. The models were ready. Jo was at her starting point on the beach and near the water's edge as the tide receded, not close enough to get her shoes wet. The scattered palm trees that marked the path toward the denser vegetation presented a challenge depending on the lighting angle. She noted that Miguel parked the device to the side, which she assumed provided the best maneuverability.

"Lara," Miguel said as he approached her with the control in hand. "The crew agreed on the camera drone's name—Clarence."

"What a hoot. Let's exercise Clarence for his aerial trial with Jo. The lighting is good and breeze perfect."

"Clarence is armed with the video camera and ready to go," Miguel added with a grin.

Lara watched Jo move, getting comfortable with the fabric and how it flowed. Miguel told all the models to loosen up before he started shooting. She was delighted Jo didn't need to be asked. The target area was beautiful and the perfect backdrop for the outfit. This outfit was earmarked for the centerpiece in the Destiny Fashion catalog and website, along with two magazines. She hoped the candid shots would get the details.

Lara watched Miguel approach Jo.

"Good morning, Jo," he said with a grin, "you look lovely. We have some side cameras taking shots, so I'm glad you were loosening up. If you don't object, I plan to use my new assistant, Clarence."

Jo nodded with a toss of her head and youthful smile. "Of course. Whatever you say."

The positive attitude and her stunning beauty had brought her fame. Miguel knew his job and pulled the best out of all her models. Lara grinned and checked a couple of items on her list.

"Thanks." Miguel directed, "Jo, go to the center and start doing the slow turns, arms out and in like an invitation. You know the routine."

Even from thirty feet away, Lara enjoyed the filming process, and Jo touched a special place in her heart. She saw Miguel step to his chair and retrieve the controller. *This is going to be electrifying,* she thought. Miguel switched Clarence on and kept his eye on Jo.

One second, Lara observed Jo smiling broadly. Then her stomach churned when Jo's eyes filled with terror as the whirling blades of the drone above and behind seemed to have startled her. Jo's reaction was unexpected when she repeatedly screamed.

"DRONES. The drones are coming!" Tears streamed down Jo's cheeks. The young girl wrapped her arms over her head, crouching. "I can't let them see me. Don't you understand I won't go back?"

It felt like time stopped. Stunned, Lara stood, ready to go to Jo, when the terrified girl spun in wild circles as if looking for something.

"I'll never go back!" she screeched, repeating the mantra as she ran toward an opening in the dense foliage.

Lara looked around. The other models, crew, and camera operator froze. One confused model murmured, "What happened?"

Lara blinked, confused, but rapidly regained her wits and refocused on her production responsibilities. She calmly told the crew, "We'll skip using the drone with Jo. Let's stage the next model."

JJ was beside Lara, looking shocked.

Lara gripped his arm. "I'm not sure what happened or what to do other than find her, JJ."

"I think I may have an idea."

"This might be a good time to do the white knight in shining armor. Find her and coax her back. Please. Tell her I'm sorry."

"Yes, Aunt Lara." He followed the path Jo disappeared into.

Less than half an hour later, he discovered Jo crouching in a thicket, her eyes still wild with fright. Shaking, she had her arms wrapped around her body. JJ sat as close as possible beside her. He caressed her hair with one hand and wrapped his other around her shoulder.

"Honey, I'm here. It's okay. You're with me now. Aunt Lara says she's sorry. She had no idea about the drones, did she?"

 Her sobs increased as she leaned into him. Several minutes later, her crying subsided as she gulped air and hiccupped. He handed her his handkerchief. She dabbed at her eyes, blew her nose, and inhaled.

"I'm so sorry. Lara didn't know. I only told you about the drones, but that sound is unmistakable."

"For most of us, drones are pretty common. This one has a camera, and I guess Miguel wanted the aerial shots. No one considered how you'd react. I was too far away when it startled you."

Jo shook her head. "He told me he was going to use his new assistant. I said no problem. What a mess I've made."

JJ watched her eyes fill with moisture again. "Jo, this is not the camp drone guards you escaped. Don't let that horrible experience dictate your life. They can't track you. You're safe with us and with me." He caressed one cheek. "You're such a brave girl. You told me how you cut the chip out of your hand. I'm not sure if I could do that."

JJ hugged her closer, trying to ease her trembling as she breathed erratic air gulps. "Sweetheart, take another breath and calm down. I'm here with you. I won't abandon you. Don't let past monsters rule your destiny. Face those fears. You are a winner."

Jo's face was the color of dried paste. "What do I tell them? You know because I told you everything about my past. The photographer couldn't know the aerial camera would trigger those horrible reminders of drones circling us constantly in that political prisoner camp. They spied on us, listened to private conversations, and delivered punishment. The horror of it flooded back when I heard those rotors. The models won't want to work with me. Lara won't want me as a model for her fashion line."

"First, Aunt Lara wants you. You're her star. The camera loves your face. Heck, the world loves your face and sweet disposition."

Jo groaned, "You know I can't tell anyone the truth. What am I going to do? I've let everyone down."

JJ weighed all the options he could think of. "I'm not a fan of lying to anyone on your team. They are like your extended family. The secret police can no longer accuse you of being Jovanna. We can't tell anyone outside the family that we engineered your new identity. We proved you're JoAnn Wagner. You made yourself JoW, the world's leading supermodel. Millions adore you. Especially young girls because they relate to your joy. Jovanna no longer exists. Your dream is a reality through hard work. You earned your success."

JJ noticed she absentmindedly rubbed the scar on her left hand. He took her hand and kissed it. "Don't worry. We need to think of a believable explanation." He stroked his chin and watched as she tapped her lips, thinking. "Jo, remember your manufactured identity Aunt Lara used to gain custody came with a troubled past."

"Yes."

"Your parents died for you to escape, right?"

She nodded in agreement, eyes widening. "No one can know about the camp I ran from."

"I agree. You could tell the crew a bit of a story on top of what Aunt Lara and Uncle Carlos created when they adopted you. You could explain how your family died in Puerto Rico. The building rubble was so bad from the hurricane that search and rescue teams required drones specially programmed for the task. Those drones, equipped with darts on wire spools, targeted modest debris. Then they hooked potential salvage and pulled it back so rescuers could probe further. You could say you were only trying to help move the debris when a drone accidentally darted your hand. Clarence, the aerial photo drone, brought that pain back in a rush. You can admit you experience random nightmares to this day. As a post-traumatic survivor, you ran for safety."

Jo slowly collected herself. With red, swollen eyes and puffy cheeks, she met JJ's steady, caring gaze. "Can you help me sell this? They can't know my real identity. If the deception is exposed, anyone who helped me would be in danger. I can't harm those who protected me. Lara, Carlos, and you are at the top of the list."

"Jo, I could tell them, but it'd be better if you told the story. I'll back you up." Looking deep into her eyes, he added, "You're an accomplished model and actor whenever you face the camera. Think of this as a role for a fashion shoot where you sell the outfit to fit the surroundings."

He gently wiped the random tears from her cheeks, then ran his fingertips across her silky hair.

"Honey, offer the story humbly, with sincerity so no one brings it up again. Ask for forgiveness for today. Plead with the crew not to repeat your history to anyone. Aunt Lara will reinforce that. I believe in you. They will, too."

Standing, Jo squared her shoulders, set her jaw with conviction, and brushed off her clothes. She used his handkerchief again, then handed it back with a chuckle. "I'm ready to offer my apology. I want this last session of the season to be perfect. Could you help me get back to the set? I can't let Lara down again."

They hugged for a moment. JJ held her at arm's length. "For the record, you didn't let anyone down. I'm proud you're facing this issue." JJ nuzzled her, then offered a reassuring hand for the stroll back to the location.

When Jo told the crew her story, there was more than one set of tearful eyes in the meeting. Everyone, including Carlos, became misty-eyed at her revelation. Jo begged to meet Clarence and understand his capabilities to control her fear. Miguel hesitated until JJ saw Aunt Lara give an approving nod. JJ watched her dispel her fright and hoped her panic would fade like when waking from a nightmare.

Keeping an eye on Jo, JJ quietly petitioned Lara. "I think it best if Clarence is left out of tomorrow's shoot to avoid aggravating her self-control. I think she's still struggling."

Lara nodded. "The sun for beach shots today is gone anyway. We'll go to plan B."

"I love that you always have a backup, Aunt Lara." He snickered.

She motioned everyone to gather around. "I hope everyone appreciated today's emotional roller-coaster ride. Rather than ordering everyone back to work, how about I order some high-calorie comfort food, and we binge for the rest of the day? We'll hit it hard tomorrow. Any objections? —Good, I thought not."

The next day's photoshoot started a lot smoother. Jo asked to be first on the lineup.

"Jo, are you sure you're ready? I don't want to push you too hard," Miguel asked.

"Please, it'll be good. I'm ready for this." She added her perky grin as her hands moved, her fingers pointing to her body, emphasizing her outfit. "You wouldn't want me to sit waiting 'til later and wrinkle this. I'm fine." She caught JJ's look and gave him a thumbs up.

JJ leaned in and whispered into Lara's ear, then returned a smile to Jo.

Miguel turned toward their boss, and Lara nodded her approval. He encouraged Jo with each shot, yet she knew something was off. The fears in her mind were affecting her natural smiles and creating stiff body movements.

Jo looked for JJ who approached her and motioned for a break. He hustled the near-to-tears Jo to the empty rest area.

"Jo, lighten up. Enjoy this, or the camera won't love you."

Jo hung her head in despair. "I'm so afraid of failing. I behaved foolishly yesterday and now." She swallowed and raised her chin. "What do I do?"

"Don't you dare cry! It'll ruin your makeup. I love you and believe in you," JJ cupped her face between his hands and his voice became stern. "Just do this. Stop the negative thoughts. You love this job. Show everyone you're the top model and more. If you get nervous, look toward me."

Jo glanced at the crew and other models—her friends and family. Their smiles boosted her resolve. Quickly giving him a determined hug, she danced back to the waiting crew. "Miguel, let's do this."

Cheers erupted. Glancing back, with eyes glistening, she mirrored JJ's encouraging smile.

Miguel chuckled. "There, that's the look I want. I believe it would help if you kept your thoughts on JJ while we shoot this segment. Go, girl. Do your thing. Teens worldwide love your vivacious appearance that reflects in the lens even when I shoot a pose. Let's have fun. Smile at JJ. Tease with the camera."

Jo moved like a skater gliding over perfect ice. With JJ in her mind, her moves were fluid and confident. She felt like a young Brazilian woman on the verge of success. Her comfortable, confident demeanor vibrated more potent in shot after shot. Simple directions came from Lara. They added individual and group photos with Jo highlighted. The view was echoed in the stunning pictures one after another.

Lara studied the photos of her protégé model with a critical eye. The full raven-colored mane overflowed her shoulders and framed her balanced facial features. It was shorter than when she started to live with them almost two years ago. Her thick hair shined in the sun with a slight natural wave bouncing with every pose. Lara noted that Jo's bright brown skin emphasized her glowing cocoa-colored eyes. Her stunning looks and shy manners made her the perfect teen representative for Destiny Fashions.

Lara planned for her team to lay out the catalogs before breaking for Christmas. The models worked hard to make up for the lost day. Each garment was illustrated with outstanding photos. Lara liked that Jo thanked the crew for their patience, promising o beat her fears before the new year. She hugged Miguel extra and asked for a private picture of her with Clarence. Nodding, he obliged with a flirty wink. As he turned to get the drone, Lara chuckled at the stern-faced look from her husband, Carlos, who appeared annoyed.

Miguel remarked, "Uh…Carlos, I got some dust in my eye. I promise you I have only the most honorable intentions. JoW requested a personal photo with the drone. I couldn't refuse her." He shrugged with his palms up.

Lara nudged Carlos, who almost smiled, nodding his assent.

Juan and Julie flew the models and critical crew members two days later to the Bernardes Estate in São Paulo. The others would arrive later for the holiday party. The models rested in their private quarters on the estate. Lara was on daily conference calls with the Destiny Fashions team in New York to ensure they were ready for the season magazine launch shortly after the new year.

The crew gathered in the post-production room for Lara to hand out assignments.

"Jason," she said, "These photos needed modest retouching." She handed him a folder and pointed out the imperfections.

"On it, ma'am."

"Caroline, we need new slicks assembled to send to our buyers and the pre-release pricing and ordering process. Can you and your team use what is ready to show me your ideas tomorrow morning?"

"Sure thing." Caroline rubbed her hands together. "This is our favorite part. I love the aerial pictures and have some ideas to promote them on the newer social media channels to ramp up the buzz. Can we get some commercial space for the videos?"

"Oh, I hope so," smiled Lara. "I can't wait to see what you come up with."

"Come on, team, we've got our work cut out for us." A small group of people followed her out.

Mary scooted over. "Lara, the fabric is ordered for each of the items. Most of the production will occur here. If you can give me the list of sizes by each design, I can start handing out the assignments. Did you want to cancel any of them based on the photo session?"

Lara shook her head. "They're all keepers. Thankfully. Please show me some of the color options you mentioned before the shoot. There are a couple I may want to offer in different colors."

Mary left to get her notes, and Lara fixed a cup of tea. This was a bit nerve-racking, but she needed to finish and start the designs for the next season. She added a touch of honey to her tea, regretting so much time away from Carlos during the post-production activities for the next couple of weeks. Mary returned and the color options for each of the items were selected.

"I'll bring you the final proofs before production."

"Thank you, Mary, great work."

Lara grabbed some fruit and reviewed her notes. She and Caroline met in the afternoon.

Caroline shuffled through the photos trying to select her favorites. "Lara, the photos are stunning."

"I agree. Jo's hard work will pay dividends this season."

"Yes ma'am. She has the qualities you want to represent your brand. The media loves her."

Lara ruefully grinned. "A little too much. The interview requests and offers from rivals are pouring in. Carlos is beefing up security, but visitors bombard the gates, requesting to see JoW. One journalist breached the estate's walled perimeter, claiming he only wanted an autograph."

"Oh no," Caroline rolled her eyes. "What did you tell Carlos?"

She nodded. "I said this is a good problem. Then, I had to remind him not to be too rough on the journalists. If we are, Destiny Fashions gains poor press, hurting JoW's public image."

"I'll have the team start giving some of the shots to top reporters if they promise to leave us in peace."

"Good idea, Caroline. I hope that helps. I will put Jason in charge for a few days to help finish the product. I only have a little over a week until the Christmas party. I need everyone to pitch in. Help me transform the Bernardes Estate with decorating and delicacies to enhance our Yuletide festivities."

"I'll help spread the word. I know the models will help. A few asked me yesterday if I needed anything."

"Great idea."

Jo was doing her assigned garlands in the library. She admired Lara, who was as relentless at decorating the estate for the coming holidays as she was managing the Destiny Fashions photo shoots. Like a drill sergeant in front of recruits, Lara handed out work assignments in rapid-fire order.

Jo pulled Carlos aside during a break from Lara's assignments.

"Uncle Carlos, can you give me special tutoring on… aerial drone flight control? Without letting anyone know or see us?"

"Why? We don't have to use the drones, though you did well when they were high enough. Lara said the shots were spectacular. No one wants you at unnecessary risk."

Jo looked down, shuffling her feet. "JJ asked me to face my fears that day. I want to prove to myself that I can. I want to keep it between us."

Carlos struggled to suppress a smile. "I'll help, Jo. But I think you're withholding something. Will you promise to tell me at some point?"

Jo's mischievous smile suggested a *maybe.*

JJ approached his uncle two days later in the kitchen where he went for a cup of coffee. "Uncle Carlos, any idea what's going on with Jo? You're head of security, so I thought I'd ask. When I ask Jo what's up, she replies that she's busy on a special project. She vanishes for hours at a time and deflects my questions."

"She asked for privacy and to keep her confidence. I'm helping her, but that is all you need to know. It would be best if you respected her choice. I must decline any further details. I recommend you focus on the task list from your Aunt Lara. Doing your job will help keep either of us getting our ears boxed for missing those deadlines."

"Can't you give me a hint?"

"I expect it to be a gift for Christmas if she locates the right non-poisonous reptile. They have a no-returns policy at the aquarium and won't let you bring anything back if it doesn't fit or isn't potty trained." Carlos grinned.

"I know where my dad honed his rapier-like wit to a sharp point while growing up. Fine. Don't ask me any favors, Uncle."

Mornings, Jo raced downstairs and jumped into the waiting car with Carlos. They traveled to an open area in a private park to practice with the drone. Under Carlos's tutelage, Jo learned to handle the controls to send the quadcopter in the desired direction.

"Remember," Carlos encouraged, "the drone will only obey your commands. You're seeking precision for what you are trying to accomplish."

Jo chuckled. "I want it to perform ballet in the sky."

After the fourth successful flight, meeting all the instructions perfectly, Jo grabbed the drone and did a bit of a happy dance. She hugged Carlos. "Thank you, Uncle Carlos, for teaching me the skills for flying and maneuvering. I think I'm over my fears." She almost triumphantly raised the drone, saying, "Meet Dove."

"Hello, Dove. I agree, Jo. You are an apt student and drone master at this point. Well done."

With a grin the size of a Cheshire Cat's, she asked, "Uncle Carlos, I want to learn even greater precision with Dove. Can you help me orchestrate a show, maybe with music? It needs to be perfect for the holiday party in three days."

Carlos clucked his tongue. "Is this where I get to know the details you are plotting, Jo?"

Jo glowed and quivered with excitement. "It is if you promise to help me keep my secret." Gaining self-confidence, she danced a little jig. "I need to prove something to myself by flying this drone. JJ found me the day I fell apart—poor man. I was a blubbering mess. I heard genuine caring in his words. I also learned how much he believed in me. He said he was proud of me as a person. He's so strong. I think I've spent enough time living with fear."

"For the record, I know you're a tough young woman. What is it you want to do?"

They sat down on the tailgate of Carlos's vehicle as she outlined her plans. He suggested some changes to make the delivery smoother.

"Oh, Carlos, I think it'll work. I can't wait to perfect the moves with your suggestions. Please let Lara in on my plan. She may have additional thoughts we can incorporate."

"Jo, we need to practice, and we both have homework. You do your portion; I'll complete mine. We'll try the sequence tomorrow until it's just like you want. I know Lara will support your plan."

Throwing herself into his arms like an excited child, she exclaimed, "Thank you so much, Carlos. I'm beyond grateful you both adopted me."

"You are most welcome. Let's go home. I'll pick you up in the morning. We have two days of serious practice to refine what you want."

"It'll be perfect."

Twinkling lights, ribbons and garlands, ornaments from around the world, and gifts scattered in stockings hung with care in several displays proclaimed Christmas Eve at the Bernardes Estate. Lara hustled everyone to finish the finishing touches, with JJ working the hardest.

Jo peered from the upstairs landing as friends, family, crew, and other guests drifted in, gave hugs, snagged cocktails, and then formed small groups of fun conversations. The steady flow of folks greeted one another at the buffet, piling their plates with tasty snacks. The oohs and aahs accompanied each sampling, some louder than others.

Jo's confidence soared as eyes turned when she entered the main room dressed in a festive evergreen satin party dress. Her natural beauty was enhanced with her dark hair loosely tied into a cascade of curls wound with golden ribbons. She smiled and spoke to friends as she made her way to Lara, standing with Carlos, JJ, and a couple of friends.

The two women embraced for a second in greeting. "Lara, may I borrow JJ for a little bit outside near the patio? I want to give him his Christmas gift."

"Of course, Jo." Lara smiled and gestured toward JJ.

JJ ruffled a hand through his hair and shifted his stance. Jo turned and took his hand, guiding him through the doors to the lawn. She had something clutched in her other hand.

Jo glanced over her shoulder. "Lara, you and the family are welcome to join us."

The family and guests quietly followed them outside. The air was warm and still. The full moon enhanced everything. White twinkling lights lit up the expansive lawn and glittered around the courtyard.

Jo positioned JJ. "Please stay here." She sweetly kissed his cheek, then paced almost ten meters away to a small table. It held an unidentified object draped in a red swatch of silk.

She heard a hint of trepidation when JJ called, "What're you doing, sweetheart? What's this all about?"

Jo, blocking the object from view, snagged the edge of the fabric and flung it into the air. It fluttered in the breeze, then settled on the ground. She pivoted to face JJ. Jo extended the antenna with a showman's flourish, operating the controller in her hands. Pressing the buttons and using both hands, she launched the red and white candy-cane-painted quadcopter straight into hover mode, timed to the holiday carol tunes playing through the patio speakers. Like a puppet attached to strings from a passing cloud, Jo navigated Dove toward JJ. He suspiciously eyed the approaching drone. A hush fell over the onlookers who stepped back from him.

Jo called, "Don't worry, JJ, this is Dove. She's peaceful. Not a menace at all."

Jo guided Dove into a beautifully orchestrated ballet with him as the centerpiece. The drone whirled around him and then hovered over his head. She exclaimed with a confident expression, "I wanted to show you that I can conquer my fears. With you in my life, I can do anything. Hold your hand straight out, palm up, and keep it steady."

JJ obliged. Dove swirled around him several more times, arcing higher and higher until it was stationary above him. The drone cockpit slid open and inverted, allowing a soft black velvet bag with gold and silver ribbons to drop neatly onto his outstretched palm.

Landing the drone back onto the small table, Jo set down the controller and shouted, "JJ, open your gift."

JJ opened the bag and carefully emptied the contents onto his palm. He looked up at Jo questioningly. Jo hoped a thousand incredible emotions were streaming through JJ, just like for her.

Walking toward JJ with eyes only for him, Jo loudly asked, "JJ, will you marry me? The ring is my plea, and Dove is the messenger."

JJ's eyes filled with emotion. He slowly surveyed the crowd, only now realizing they were witnesses. Deftly brushing away stray tears, he reached for her hand as she stopped beside him. "Jo, I accept this ring. I'll marry you, my love!"

JJ put on the ring and pulled Jo into a warm embrace topped with a lengthy kiss. The onlookers erupted into cheers and well wishes. The family members approached the couple.

Lara offered, "Congratulations, you two. Now, if we can complete the rest of the ceremonies, please."

JJ's head snapped around. "This isn't just a Christmas celebration?"

Lara finished his statement, "Nope, it's also a wedding party orchestrated by your amazing fiancée. Family and friends want to see you wed this Christmas Eve. Then we can crank up this party." Juan Sr. clapped his stunned son on the back and pressed another ring into his hand. "I knew you'd say yes. Your mom said this one matches the one from Jo. You come from a line of men who don't let the best woman escape. Congratulations, son."

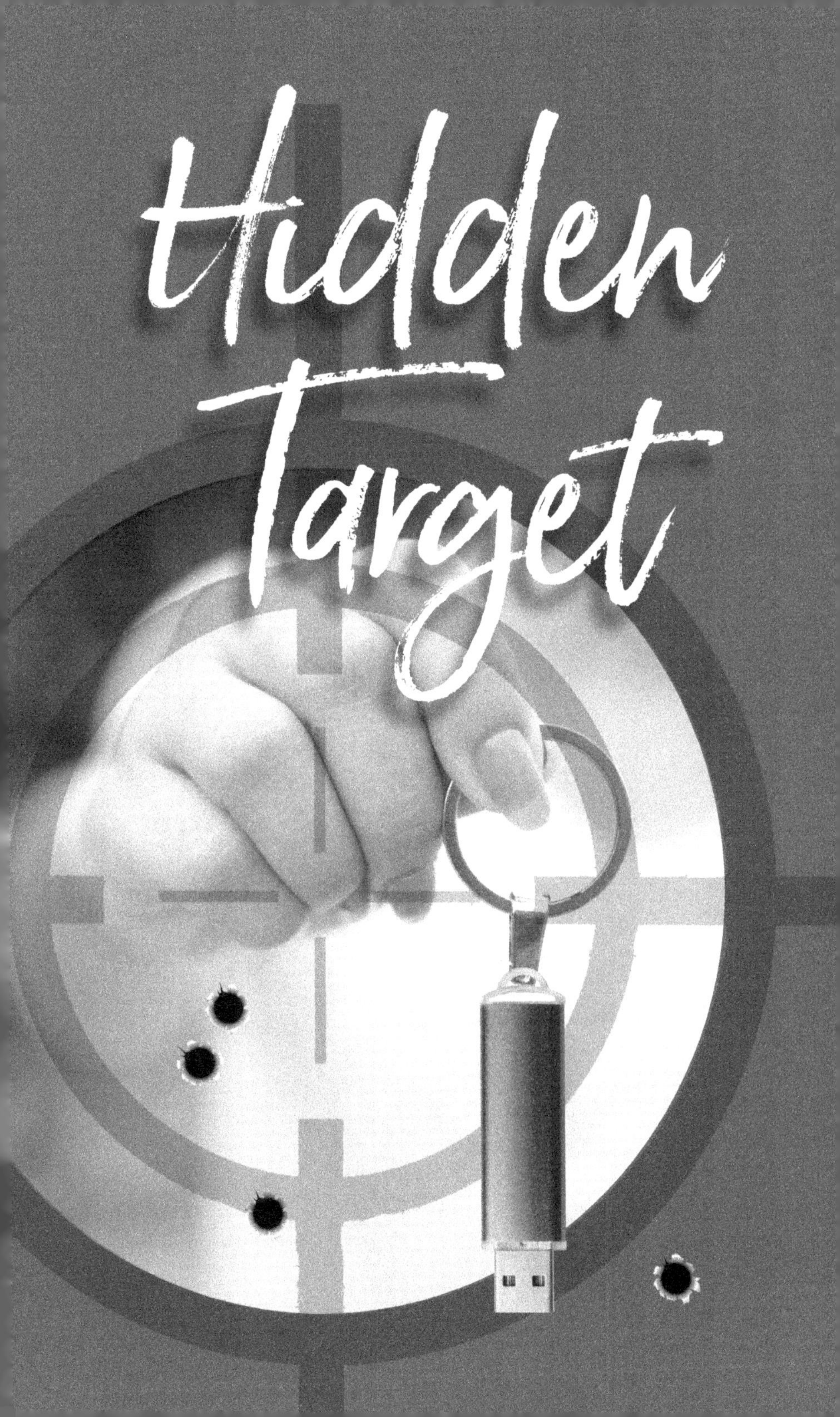
Hidden
Target

*B*rayson ducked to avoid clipping his ballcap on the six-foot opening and dropped his gear inside the cabin entry. "Whew, Renaldo was right about his place being remote." He scrolled, then clicked Renaldo's contact on his cell. It immediately connected

"Hey, buddy, arrived. Your place is remarkable, tucked away from the D.C. noise. I plan to hike the park you recommended." He moved toward the window to check out the view. "Yep. You're right about me needing the quiet to reflect. I'll get my head right before I return to crimefighting."

He checked out the contents of the refrigerator while he listened.

"Stay there as long as you want," said Renaldo. "I hope you finally realize you couldn't save Gretchen. From what you told me, in her way, she loved you, even though you never had a real relationship."

"Yep, I'm sad she's dead, but I am past trying to change the results. My therapy helped. I'll be fine, especially after spending time in your cabin. You have provided a remarkably peaceful place to get my head on straight. Thanks again."

He disconnected the call, pocketed the device in his shirt pocket, and combed his longish dark hair with his fingers.

Grabbing his worn, brown canvas bag, he inspected the interior. He added the ballcap and stored the remainder of his meager belongings in one of the bedrooms. He went back to the car and secured the cooler. Emptying the contents for two weeks' worth of wining and dining into the refrigerator and one cabinet, he caught sight of the electric coffee pot. "That's perfect," he muttered with a grin. "I hope there's coffee and filters."

He opened the cabinet, finding the needed items, plus cups. Glancing out the window over the sink, he spotted the barbeque through the window, envisioning a steak soon. Finished touring the space, he spotted the trophy from one of Renaldo's previous hunts. "Hello, Clifford. Guess we're roommates. You're my muse," he mumbled to the mounted antelope. "I'm headed out for target practice. You hang tight; I'll be back."

He grabbed his range bag to verify its contents. "Rats," he groused, "I forgot my spotting scope. Maybe I can borrow one."

Brayson secured the cabin, noting the details of the surrounding area. He jumped into the Jeep and plugged the range address into his phone. Focused on the road, he said, "Midday cruising with no traffic, I like it." The oak trees on both sides of the road boasted big leaves. "I bet the colors are brilliant in the fall. Perhaps I can return to enjoy the season."

After he parked, Brayson spotted a few shooters practicing in the designated areas by distance. The familiar scent of burnt gunpowder tickled his nose. He entered the store, seeing ammunition, hunting gear, and the counter to purchase range time. A burly man smiled as he approached.

"Howdy." The man extended his hand. "Name's Joe Briggs, the owner. How ya doing?"

"I'm Brayson Morris," he introduced with a smile. They firmly shook.

"Mr. Briggs, I'd like to schedule time in your long-range area to dial in my 300-magnum and purchase two boxes of shells. I could buy a spotting scope unless you have one to rent."

Joe nodded, but his smile vanished. as he reached for the shells. He raised an eyebrow and questioned, "Did you need shooting earmuffs, too?"

"Thanks, Joe, that'd be better than just my earplugs."

Joe turned his head and, over his shoulder, called, "Marian, can you spot on the range for this gentleman?"

Brayson's attention shifted when a pretty woman emerged from a passageway behind the counter.

"Sure, Joe," she replied in a friendly tone.

Brayson noticed her brightly scrubbed face, blonde hair knotted tight on top of her head, and enigmatic expression. His eyes roved from head to toe, guessing her height at five feet six inches. Even camouflaged by oversized jeans and a bulky flannel shirt, she reminded him of a sure-footed cat, pure female, as she approached the counter.

Joe glared at him with a pointed, no-nonsense look. "Marian can spot for you. You appear a nice enough guy. But I don't know you, so let me have your ID."

Brayson quickly delivered his license and credit card. "I won't need a spotter, just a 200-yard or more location."

Joe ran a quick check on his computer and rang up the sale. He passed the receipt across the counter for signature. "You're either highly distracted or rusty to forget ear protection and a scope. I added a deposit for the scope," he said as he handed it over from under the counter. "Marian will ensure you pose no risk to the other folks using my range."

Rubbing his face with frustration, Brayson replied, "Point taken. The verification should have told you that I'm a qualified shooter with a military background." He stuffed the shells and scope into his bag and grabbed the paper targets paid with the range fee. Then he stomped toward the door, shaking his head as he glanced over his shoulder. "Come on, Marian. Could you point me to my station? Please."

"Yes, sir," she responded, adding a sarcastic salute ending with her index finger across the tip of her nose.

Marian assisted with the sandbags at their station. After the range officer nodded, Brayson headed toward the designated frames and stapled the targets.

When he returned, the range officer barked, "Range is hot!"

Brayson's first three shots barely hit in the black, nowhere close to the bullseye. Annoyance following the insinuations of Joe messed with his concentration. He stretched as he rolled his shoulders.

Looking through her scope, Marian, on his right, told him, "Low and to the left by eight centimeters. Hold your weapon slightly higher and to the right unless you're sighting to let your opponent live."

Even with her precise vocal corrections, his shooting didn't improve with bursts of five rounds of three shots. Amidst his growing irritation with successive misses to center, Brayson asked, "Hey, Marian, can you look at my weapon? The sighting seems off."

Marian approached and beamed as she held out her hand for the weapon. She checked the weight and got a sense of the balance before loading the gun. She set her stance to shoot.

Recognizing her skill with the gun, he told her, "Shoot the new target on the right. I'll spot."

She slowly breathed and didn't rush. Her fluid movements with the bolt-action rifle suggested extensive experience. Brayson was stunned after her fifth shot followed the others dead center, with the bullseye hole barely expanded.

Marian returned the weapon with a broad smile and dancing eyes. "Great weapon. Shoots nice."

"You're a good shot. Getting humiliated on the range wasn't in my plan today," He admitted.

She shrugged her shoulders and raised her palms. "Beginner's luck."

He laughed. "Next, you'll tell me you're George Washington in disguise." Amused at his light joke, he added, "Are you in the habit of being gracious when salvaging bruised egos? The only people I've seen shoot like you were sniper-trained graduates. I didn't qualify. Should I call you Master Gunnery Sergeant Marian?"

"Try a few more shots before you run home to Mrs. Morris."

He ignored her comment but sensed the familiar distancing of emotions buried in her comment. He was the poster boy for that club, but being alone too much wasn't healthy, as he learned with his recent therapy. He loaded the weapon and fired a few more rounds, getting closer to the center. He glanced at her wryly and said, "There's no Mrs. Morris, Maid Marian."

She bristled like a dog who'd discovered an intruder. "Maid Marian?" She placed her hands on her hips and jutted her chin up. "Where's that coming from?"

He aimed, fired, then commented, "There's no ring on your finger. No makeup. You dress to be unattractive. Plus, your long hair is in a librarian bun like you're trying to imitate a mouse. If I knew you better, I'd ask why."

"I'll bet you forgot your cleaning kit, too," she countered with an unmistakable smirk.

He caught the sarcastic tone and stance of a woman who wouldn't take crap off anyone.

"Let's clean your friend's weapon before you return it. There's nothing worse than someone borrowing a weapon and returning it dirty. Come on."

They found a tabletop to spread out the towel to set the pieces on. Brayson fumbled as he field-stripped the weapon. Marian grunted, grabbed the rifle, and expertly disassembled it. She removed the gunpowder residue and, with a practiced hand, applied a light coating of gun oil. She reassembled the weapon like a specialist and handed it back. Brayson nodded his thanks as Joe wandered toward them.

"Looks like you had a good session judging from the targets." Shifting his attention toward Marian, he added, "Kid, I've got to work late. A group called to reserve the range after hours. They're paying extra. I can't give you a lift home. You're welcome to stay and help, but it'd be on your own time."

Disappointment registered on Marian's face. Before she responded, Brayson offered, "No worries, I'll drop you off. It's the least I can do after your expert shooting lessons."

Joe laughed. "I'm willing to bet, Marian, that after watching you shoot, his intentions are honorable."

● ● ●

An awkward silence filled the Jeep for the first few minutes after she supplied the directions. As the void expanded, Brayson realized he wanted to learn more about her. "Marian, I got off on the wrong foot earlier. I've some issues I need to fix. You were helpful today, thank you."

The dam of silence crumbled, allowing them to chat amicably for the remainder of the ride. Brayson turned into her apartment complex and parked. They got out. He looked around, mentally cataloging the models of the cars, lack of sounds, and random decorations on apartment doors.

He paused and remarked, "Which one is yours? Tell me it's not the one with the open door."

She bolted from the car, and he trailed her up the stairs as she dashed to the open doorway. Marian stood stock-still, staring into her efficiency space, her fists clenched. "Tossed, dammit." She stormed inside. "He found me, Ha, but he missed the prize."

Brayson saw Marian swipe at the unwanted tears, then grasp the chain at her neckline. She walked through to the open closet and grabbed a duffle. He remained quiet as she methodically added contents to the pouch.

Seeing a smashed picture frame near her, he bent to pick it up. The photo depicted Marian in her Air Force uniform decorated with ribbons through the fractured glass. Her smile radiated her pride in that moment.

"Don't bother trying to clean." She said, restraining his arm. "He'll be back." She pointed to the words scribbled on the kitchen wall. "See the note? I've got to run fast and light. My life's a mess." She sighed. "My memories are my keepsakes. I'm sorry you had to see this. You don't want to be involved."

She added the photo at the last second, closed the bag, and made a beeline for the door, but he snagged her arm.

"Hold up, Marian. You've got a stalker who wants something, and you plan to strike out on foot? Give me your case." In a softer tone, he added, "You're coming with me. I want to help."

Marian inhaled. "You seem like a nice guy, even if you're a poor shot. You don't want in this. This guy is an unforgiving badass I hoped would never find me." Her hand swept across the mess around them. "I'm not a damsel in distress. I did two tours and can take care of myself."

He smiled and stared into her pretty, troubled face. "Then consider me your squad member. I'm here to take you back to base. Move it, sister!"

She brightened with a saucy grin and handed him the case. He watched her rush to the freezer and pull out a bag labeled vegetables. She opens her field knife and cuts a shallow hole for the entire length. Then she removed passports along with a sizeable greenback wad. She stuffed these into her deep jacket pocket and returned to his side. "Now we can leave."

Brayson glanced outside and observed no movement. His body shielded hers while one arm encircled her waist as they made their way to the Jeep. Opening the door, she melted into the passenger floorboard to hide. He rounded to the driver's side, entered, and started the engine.

"Take a left out of the parking lot and a right at the third street a right," she relayed. "We're headed to the Interstate."

"Perfect. I'm staying at a place tucked in the woods about forty or so minutes from here."

"Let's make certain you aren't followed."

He circled twice. Confident they had no tail, he set his trip to navigate toward Renaldo's place. Reaching over, he tapped her head. "You can get up. No traffic anywhere."

Marian sat in the seat and buckled her belt. "Thanks. Seems like you've been in this sort of movie before. You aren't married, you're fit, and you think on multiple planes, like ex-military. Who are you?"

Memories of work throughout his life played in his mind. He caught her profile. "Yeah, I've seen similar scenarios in many reruns—some military. I'm a champ at securing popcorn and drinks without missing the action scenes. But let's start with your mess. Who's after you, and why? A jilted lover?"

She snorted as she dragged her fingers through flyaway strands of hair. "After the Air Force, I wanted a life of love, success, and family. I met Mister Wonderful, who I thought was the man of my dreams, in a coffee shop. I attributed his intensity and gregarious conversation to way too much coffee. He asked what I wanted to do. When I didn't have a good answer, he provided one. He showed me his profitable business."

Brayson glanced her way to see any emotion but remained silent.

She snorted and shifted in her seat. "Here's the condensed version. Wonderful planted software trojans on point-of-sale devices and harvested credit card information. Did you realize the underworld slimeballs sell credit card numbers with pins on the Darknet for up to a hundred dollars each? He had thousands. He stole identities and social security numbers to hock in his free time for a lot more. Value-added activities like this allow a seller to advance from petty cybercriminals to wholesale cyber-brokers. That's who's hunting me."

He shook his head and shrugged, recognizing the type. "Sounds like a copycat of Dread Pirate Roberts of Silkroad fame. That extortionist is serving life in federal prison. What exactly did you do to get his wrath?"

She grinned. "I copied all the files from his laptop and launched a disk wipe program to prevent data recovery." She laughed. "He might also be a little angry because I took his stash of freezer cash." He noted she grinned like a cat who licked the last drop of cream. "I guess some folks don't see the humor in discovering their money is gone and their machine got trashed."

He laughed. "Understandable."

"That's my story." She smiled with a slight look of relief. "And you," she smugly asked, "what's your black ops story? And what did the lady do to you?"

Collecting his thoughts, Brayson executed another exit hop, checking for followers. "Odd how the universe works. I'm on a forced leave of absence from a cyber security team. And you need the same services we deliver."

He spotted her eyebrows raise as if interested. "Hmm. I trust you're better at fixing digital issues than distance shooting?"

He groaned in annoyance as he reentered the Interstate.

"I'm just wondering if I'm safe," she quipped.

"I think you are. I'm pretty good at my job," he said as he refocused on the road. "I met Gretchen in college in Europe. She was brilliant, stunning, and aloof. She left after one semester. We were friends. I would have liked more, but her family controlled her agenda. We crossed paths a few months ago when I was on a case. Again, she came in and out of my life—a broken woman no one could help. I'll save the rest of the details for another time. We're approaching my turn. I'll stop and watch. If no vehicles appear interested, we go."

They paused an extra five minutes before he continued. He pulled behind the cabin before stopping the engine. Exiting, he lifted her bag and caught her attention. "Hey, this isn't a hinky deal. This cabin has two bedrooms, and one's all yours. You need help, and I want your slime-boy behind bars. If you're willing to share your info on Mister Wonderful, I've got friends who'd like to make that happen."

She nodded as they entered. Brayson gestured to the spare room toward the open room. She went in and put her stuff away. Returning to the kitchen, following the aroma of brewed coffee, she sat "Whatcha got in mind?"

He poured them each a cup.

She ignored the additives in the center of the table. Taking a sip, Marian groaned with pleasure. "Heavenly flavor. Glad you make great coffee."

"You've got something he wants. The note said he'll get you." Brayson watched her face when he offered, "You could return everything to him and vanish using one of your phony IDs. I'd like to know how to find you if I ever send out Christmas cards."

"All right. My name is Marian Hays; the extra passports are for traveling incognito. I picked up a cloaking technique from Mister Wonderful, Timofey Kalashnik, or Timosha as he prefers. He said Kalashnik meant bread maker, which suits his cyber scum business. I want to put him away and live my life."

They sipped in companionable silence until Brayson decided they needed to eat while he pondered how best to offer his help. He popped open chicken soup and heated it on the gas stove. Pulling out crackers, he filled a plate and set it between them. The aromatic, steamy mixture, he thought, was always good for what ailed someone. He ladled two mugs to the rim, grabbed spoons and napkins, then placed the items on the table.

"We need to eat."

In between bites, Brayson sent a text message to Renaldo. Several heartbeats later, he received a response. He read it twice, astonished at the content. "Wow!"

He looked at her with a grin. "Maid Marian, Timosha is wanted for all kinds of naughty indiscretions. As luck would have it, he's illegally on U.S. soil."

Marian dropped her spoon. Her face contorted with fear and surprise. "Who's your FBI contact?"

"We stick to saying three-letter agencies as they each have their place in law enforcement. My buddy will be here early tomorrow, and he can introduce himself then. In the meantime, I'd like to see what you've got on the USB drive on your necklace." Brayson arched an eyebrow. "I'm good at observation and lucky guessing."

Marian's features formed a scowl at getting bested. "Damn, you saw my quick check at the apartment."

"Look, Maid Marian, I see two scenarios. One, you're delusional, and this is a fairy tale. You tossed your apartment, and no one is after you, making you a cruel con artist. Or, you have his data, and he wants to hurt you. Getting his stuff back won't help you in the least." Brayson tilted his head and watched her eyes searching for a clue to her integrity. "I'm inclined to believe the latter. I'd like to see some proof. I'm too old to work with anyone I can't trust. It's up to you."

Marian stared defiantly into his steady gaze, then pulled out her necklace and extended it. Brayson powered up his laptop and inserted the device. After the automatic virus scan, he opened the spreadsheet. He studied several pages of the massive file and gazed into her bottomless green-blue eyes. "Wow. I'd love to hear the part when you discovered he was nothing but a cyber thief. There looks like thousands of credit card numbers, grouped by retail outlets, sorted by dollars purchased, and aggregated for sale to his client list. You're not wrong; he's a Darknet cyber wholesaler of stolen numbers. You forgot to tell me the part where he accepted pre-payment from affiliates of the Russian Hydra group."

Marian shook her head as the veins pulsed on her forehead. "Hydra? What's that?"

"Hydra's a closed group or Darknet organization that vets members to validate they're not police. Hydra is where one goes to buy or offer assassinations, narcotics, weapons, prostitution, purchase inventory for human trafficking—anything illegal. Hydra takes a cut from all transactions with payment in cryptocurrency."

Marian blinked, looking worried. "Oh no. I stole from Timosha, who owes goods to this Hydra group. They probably have no sense of humor either."

"I guess we'll take a raincheck on the wine and steak I thought we'd eat later. Let's sleep in shifts as a precaution. I'll text my contact these details. I predict a pre-dawn breakfast party."

Marian stood and paced. "Why are you helping? You hardly know me."

Brayson recalled how he failed Gretchen, even though he couldn't change the outcome. "I've got a soft spot for strong, independent women. I'd like to see you get the life you want. I'll take the first watch."

It was still dark when Brayson's phone chirped. He rose and opened the door to Renaldo and his crew. Marian greeted everyone and handed over the thumb drive.

Renaldo inserted it into his laptop and reviewed the data. He whistled low. "Nice work, ma'am. This drive is not only worth millions, but it contains detailed contacts. We'll be busy for months." He rubbed his hands together with a delighted expression.

Brayson decided his friend looked like a kid in a candy shop. "Do you have enough to run a sting operation without Marian and me?"

"With this much bait and knowing where to poke Hydra, you two can drift out of town with a clear conscience. I'll arrange the transport to anywhere. Keep an eye on the news for Timosha's arrest."

Brayson smiled and faced Marian. "Looks like we made it, Maid Marian. Go where you want. Have your life. Renaldo will deliver something far better than a bus ticket."

Marian's smile faded as Brayson added, "Thanks for helping, Renaldo. I've got my transport and plan to leave in the morning. It's time I returned to work in Luxemburg. Appreciate your handling everything."

"Marian, it's been festive. You've helped me immeasurably. Perhaps our paths will cross again." He grasped her hand, amazed at the unexpected flash of sensation coursing through his body. He shook it off with a pleasant smile.

Late the next day, after the long flight, Brayson dropped his gear inside his apartment. He sighed. "It feels good to be back home," he said aloud. He mixed a drink, turned on the radio to quiet jazz, and headed to the couch to relax, staring out the window at the twinkling lights. A knock intercepted his relaxation. He opened the door. His greeting stopped into open-mouth silence.

Marian smirked and cocked her head. "You meant it when you told Renaldo to take me wherever I wanted, right? I want to explore the electric jolt between us."

Grinning, he nodded. "Come on in. But I've only got one bedroom."

She folded into his open arms. "Good."

*W*olfgang sipped the last of his brandy, enjoying the flames flickering in the fireplace. He shifted in the armchair and stretched his slippers toward the warmth, grateful for the cushiony soft leather. The warm library invited lively conversation, games, and sipping fine wines or spirits with couches, chairs, and tables scattered about. Some might consider it formal with the valuable antiques and artwork, but his family often commented it felt comfortable. Tonight's chess game with Jacob was outstanding. With his win tonight, Jacob had played even better than his mother, Julianna. Jacob recalled a few stories from when his Granny, Adrianna, lived with him and his mother.

Wolfgang tried not to dwell on things of the past because it made him feel old and sad. When it was late, too quiet, and sleep wouldn't come, his mind drifted. He'd recall the one event he wished he could change. It wasn't his fault. Nothing could have altered the outcome. For three decades, the nagging what-ifs had persisted. He reminded himself that Jacob, his grandson, was with him. The young man, grown before they met, looked like him with his thick dark hair, blue eyes, and lean stature. That had to be enough. Wolfgang was relieved Jacob hadn't pushed for details of his life in Europe in the 1960s. The times were different, with the remnants of war buried in the shadows of time.

Knowing he wouldn't sleep for hours, Wolfgang let his mind drift and recalled his vibrant, brilliant daughter, Julianna, laughing with his wife and only love, Adrianna. Both women were of medium height, lithe, and had wavy, flowing dark hair gracing their backs. Dresses were shorter than ever yet stylish and moved around them. Casual onlookers might think them sisters. Their laughter and chatter filled the air when they were together.

Wolfgang, good with numbers, made his living in the financial market. At the end of WWII, he and two friends also established a secretive family business under the umbrella of the R-Group. The goal was to establish a legacy for their children. To prepare them, they invested in extensive private tutoring.

He and Adrianna fiercely loved and protected their only child, Julianna. She was home-schooled except for the two years she attended a private women's university. They carefully cultivated activities to expand her knowledge and satiate her curiosity. She thrived in this exclusive education, studying sciences, mathematics, history, literature, finances, new technologies, and fluency in multiple languages. Social interactions were limited to extended family events, including a few cousins, though she was the eldest. The family business activities were not shared due to the dark cloud of the Soviet Iron Curtain hanging over Europe. The specialized business prepared for an uncertain future even while expanding the support to honest governments, businesses, and people.

Like her father, Julianna happily focused on study, travel, and work, honing her talents with logic and numbers. She was a happy, obedient youth who met her obligations with a smile.

"Father, I'd like a job at the bank. Are there any openings? I want to be as good in finance as you." Julianna asked with a smile during dinner a week after she finished college.

He picked up a bit of their dinner on his fork and glanced at his wife, who grinned, clearly aware of their daughter's plan. "You've finished your education and are ready to take on the world?"

She swallowed with a reflective expression. "I'm not certain about the world, but I'd like the responsibility. I doubt the learning will ever end. I'd rather gain practical experience from you both. Mother works part-time and mentioned she wouldn't mind working more hours."

"Ah, the two of you are in on this," he admitted after looking between the pair.

He recalled as if he still felt the touch as Adrianna reached over and patted his arm. "You know us so well, sweetheart. It might do her good while she figures out what she wants to do."

"We have talked about having a concierge of sorts to greet people. It would require you to learn everyone's job to direct or escort people to the right resource." He raised an eyebrow, watching for her reaction.

"Yes, Father, that sounds perfect. When can I start?"

"Tomorrow," he said, his heart filled with pride in her. "We can ride together, and your mother can get those extra hours learning the computer applications we're installing."

He heard their unison, "Perfect."

Julianna worked hard from her first day to learn each person's job. Her knack for details and offers to help endeared her to the other bank employees. A desk near the entrance kept her in his line of sight as she greeted customers and directed them to the correct area to complete their transactions. She often recalled their name on subsequent visits. Everyone liked her cheerful demeanor and helpful nature. One afternoon, a young, well-dressed man entered the establishment. Wolfgang heard that initial exchange.

"Good afternoon, sir. My name is Julianna; how can I help you?"

"Good afternoon," he said, "I need to open up some new accounts for my expenses. I have a line of credit document."

Wolfgang saw the man hand her a document. He observed her reviewing the paper with a slight wrinkle on her forehead.

"Let me check with my manager, just a moment, please."

She strode into Wolfgang's office and handed him the document. "Sir," she softly spoke, "he wants to open accounts. I'm not familiar with the agent for his credit. What do I do?"

"Send him in, please. I'll take care of it."

During Wolfgang's first meeting with Andreas Müller, the young man seemed attentive and even formal during their exchange. But he recollected something felt off, but nothing out of the ordinary arose during the standard background checks. Establishing the two accounts, he passed a small book of checks and a savings register. Unconvinced that Andreas was who he seemed, Wolfgang vowed to complete some additional inquiries. They rose and exchanged a formal handshake. With a brief nod of thanks, Andreas squared his shoulders, turned, and walked toward the exit.

Wolfgang's eyes followed his path to the desk of his daughter. The young man smiled as Julianna stood. He extended a hand, which Julianna clasped, and he covered with his other. "Thank you for your assistance. I've opened accounts and look forward to seeing you whenever I have a transaction."

"Good. I'm glad you were successful," she said, extracting her hand, though a smile and flushed cheeks spoke of her interest. "Have a nice day."

Wolfgang fought the urge to warn his daughter of his concerns. He'd seen other parents within his social circle do this, resulting in rebellious children. One youth had committed suicide, while another ran away. He shared his worries with Adrianna later that evening. They agreed that to try to force anything on Julianna at her age was a mistake. They would maintain a watchful eye while they supported their daughter's first taste of attention.

The weekly reports Wolfgang reviewed confirmed Andreas' accounts showed modest transactions. He returned often to complete his transactions. At every opportunity, he requested Julianna's help. Each visit included additional conversations, teasing banter, and a walk during lunch.

Several days later, during dinner that night, Julianna asked, "Mother, Andreas Müller asked me to take a walk tomorrow through the park. I want your approval."

"I've seen him in the bank, always making time for you. I'm not surprised, but, darling girl, we don't know his family. I am fine with you taking a walk, but I must follow as a precaution," Adrianna offered.

Julianna frowned but then nodded.

"I won't intrude on the conversation. I'll keep my distance," she said, crossing her heart. "I promise. It's not to embarrass you but to protect you."

"Yes, ma'am."

The next day began the first of many private walks and meals. Wolfgang relaxed his concerns as Andreas selected public settings. At no time were they unchaperoned. Julianna never complained nor suggested Andreas had a problem with the arrangement.

Adrianna shared with her inexperienced daughter the reality of wealthy European families maintaining social traditions. Young women were not as restricted as before the war, yet a lady's honor was valued. Her behavior reflected on the family and their business reputations. Julianna and this lad spent weeks strolling in the local park. Adrianna accompanied them at a discreet distance. A handful of weeks later, Julianna set her cup aside and cleared her throat. "Father, Mother, I believe Andreas Müller is the one for me. I want him as a life partner so I can be as happy as you both."

Wolfgang warmed to Julianna's twinkling eyes, recalling his courting years and joy at his choice. Adrianna squealed with delight and reached across the table, squeezing her daughter's fingers as her eyes glistened.

"Has he proposed to you?"

"No, Father. I want him to come to dinner and get to know us as a family. I know you'll approve once you get to know him. He's nice to me and makes me laugh. Father, you may have found a new challenger for chess."

The shadow of doubt crossed his mind. "Good, he's being respectful.

"We'll have him to dinner and cook a fabulous meal so he can know how capable you are," Adrianna proclaimed.

They agreed.

Julianna clapped with excitement with a grin that lit up the room. "How about the day after tomorrow." She bit the side of her thumb. "Does that give us enough time?"

"You may invite him," Wolfgang agreed.

Wolfgang enjoyed the activity that consumed most of Saturday as his beautiful wife and daughter chuckled while fixing special treats for their dinner guest, Andreas.

The aroma of their creations filled the air, promising mouth-watering choices for dinner, especially the desserts. Through the years, he savored all the dishes Adrianna created and was grateful she'd taken the time to tutor Julianna in cooking and other helpful household skills. The chateau had a staff who learned long ago they were all considered an extended family.

Wolfgang recalled overhearing a portion of the conversation that made him smile.

"Darling, when I told your grandparents about your father, they were appalled," Adrianne began. "Of course, I hadn't yet turned eighteen, and he was older. My mother stuck to me like glue until the wedding day."

"Mother, I had no idea you were so young. I loved your wedding pictures. Do you still have the dress?"

"I do, and it will fit you like a second skin."

That evening at the appointed time, Wolfgang greeted Andreas at the door. Dinner was a huge success, with delicious Polish dishes and lively conversation. The young man was quick-witted and told wonderful stories they enjoyed. Wolfgang felt he was attentive to ladies. Andreas challenged him to a chess game when they retired to the library. He lost but seemed to accept the defeat with grace, promising a rematch at some point. The evening extended with coffee and stories of various family adventures.

Andreas appeared lost in thought, sipping his coffee, then looked at Wolfgang. "Mr. and Mrs. Mickelowski, I'd like your permission for Julianna to visit my parents' country home near Lake *Zürich*. A small group is joining us for the weekend to celebrate the birthday of my best friend, Iwan. Our chateau is large enough for an extended weekend holiday, perfect for the younger crowd. Two young ladies Julianna knows sent their acceptance notes this morning."

"Though it sounds exciting, I," Adrianna said, focusing her blue eyes on her husband, "we've never met your parents."

Andreas nodded. "Few local families have met my parents. We've only recently moved to the estate on the lake. I'm not certain how to get you together before this party."

"Julianna, do you know the girls who accepted, and do we know their parents?" asked Wolfgang.

"I don't know. Honestly, this is the first I've heard about a get-together." Julianna turned toward Andreas.

"I'm sorry, Julianna. I didn't want to mention anything until I met your parents. The young ladies are Maria Schneider and Linnea Tanner, who have been to the chateau for daytime events. You've mentioned them to me during our chats."

"Oh, great. Mother, I first met them at university. I'm sure you know their mothers."

Adrianna nodded and smiled. "Yes, I do. Young man, let me speak with them. Can Wolfgang call you tomorrow afternoon?"

"Of course, no problem." He wiped his mouth and laid his napkin to the side of the silver spoon and bone china cup and saucer. "I need to be going."

The group moved toward the door, and Andreas turned. "Thank you for the magnificent meal. I look forward to hearing from you tomorrow."

Wolfgang felt his heart tug when Julianna kissed them good night and wiggled her fingers as she glided upstairs to bed.

Wrapping his arm around Adrianna, he returned with her to the library to chat before they retired. They settled on the couch with brandy. He warmed the ambrosia with his hands and said, "I'm not certain this a good idea, honey."

"I'm not either, but she is at an age where she can choose. Further, she's asked permission and sought our approval. We're very fortunate. He does seem to check all the boxes, and his manners are impeccable."

"Agreed, but …"

"Unless something changes, we'll respect her wishes if this is who she wants. Let me call around tomorrow and see if I can get information from the girls' mothers and others we know. I want to know his parents, not simply see their balance sheet."

The next day, Adrianna entered Wolfgang's office with a lunch tray and closed the door.

"Thank you for lunch. What did you discover?" he asked.

"I spoke with Maria's mother, who indicated that she had met the Müllers in town when they purchased the house. After the family moved in, she and other ladies in the area were invited to a luncheon at the estate. The house was opulent and well-staffed. Maria's mother indicated she enjoyed her conversation with Mrs. Müller. They discussed art, fashion, and Mrs. Müller's passion for travel. Andreas travels for business, which aligns with his transactions and transfers to his accounts here. However, after that, she never visited with the Müller family. They were sometimes gone for weeks at a time on trips."

"If Andreas' parents are gone that much, does that mean they won't be home during the celebration?"

"I don't know how we might check that. Oh, and the Müllers paid cash for the estate, which is well-maintained. How senior Müller earns his income was unclear, but likely consulting."

"Are the other girls going?"

"Yes, and Linnea's mother, who also attended the luncheon, thought they would be well protected with all the staff."

"All right. What if we convince Julianna to bring our maid Crissy to help with gowns and hair?"

"I think that works. She'll have someone she can trust if needed. Plus, it's a four-day weekend. Plans include sailing, horseback riding, walks on the lake, meals, and two dances with live bands."

Wolfgang walked to the door. He opened it and signaled to Julianna. She rushed in, appearing hopeful.

"Darling girl, your father and I would like to meet his parents as soon as possible, but we approve of your taking advantage of the invitation. We know you'll have fun and maybe get some new friends. You must bring Crissy to attend to your clothing and hair."

Wolfgang was glad he closed the door to his office door when she squealed.

She rushed to hug them. "Thank you. May I call him from your phone, Father?"

"Of course, I need to work on my report."

Julianna appeared ecstatic and blushed when she called. "Andreas, I have permission to attend. I'm bringing one of my maids, which I hope won't be a problem."

Her head nodded, and a smile grew from his side of the discussion. She handed the phone to her father.

Wolfgang was reassured by Andreas' plan to pick up the two other young ladies a week from Friday in the morning in his car before stopping there. He promised Julianna would call when they arrived.

The event went as advertised. Julianna returned home at midday on Monday. During their evening discussion, she regaled them with details. She even brought her diary to reference each activity.

"The estate is almost as lovely as ours. Lush green manicured lawns and meandering flower gardens with seasonal blooms bursting out colors from brilliant white to purple. The view of Lake *Zürich* from the patio beckoned a walk along the shore or taking a boat for a lazy row across the rippling water. We did all those things."

"It sounds magnificent. And your accommodations?" asked Wolfgang.

"The whole interior had tastefully appointed rooms, elegantly decorated with Turkish rugs, French paintings, and furniture from around the world, inviting sitting and conversation."

"Wolfgang, perhaps one day we can see it ourselves." Adrianna sighed.

Julianna spent another hour on the party atmosphere, meals, and delightful conversations.

"Mother, I know I'm in love. Can we include Andreas in more of our family dinners? He said he wanted a rematch at chess, Father."

"Certainly, he's welcome in our home as long as he treats you like the treasure you are.

Wolfgang observed the lovebirds walking hand-in-hand in the chateau's gardens the following Saturday night dinner. They enjoyed lively conversation, delicious meals, and chess at subsequent meals over the next handful of weeks. Wolfgang wasn't won over, like Adrianna, but he was warming to the young man. He admitted Andreas had a business head, even though his exact business ventures remained unclear. At one point deflecting the answer, Andreas confided his enterprises were extremely top secret.

On a moonlit evening six months later, Wolfgang watched out the window as Julianna and Andreas strolled along the paths. They paused at one of the benches to enjoy the scents and muted sounds of the garden. Andreas took her hand and knelt before her. He called to Adrianna to watch. They saw him slipping a ring that caught the moonlight reflected onto Julianna's finger.

Her face painted with surprise and delight, Julianna threw her arms around him, saying something they could only imagine through the glass.

Acting surprised when the ecstatic couple returned to the library to share the news, Wolfgang winced at his lingering reservations about Andreas. The happiness reflected in the eyes of his daughter won him over. She was an adult. He graciously gave them his blessing and opened a bottle of champagne so they could share a toast to the future.

Weeks passed while plans for the wedding progressed. Wolfgang realized they had grown lax in their vigilance. Julianna was away more in the evenings with Andreas alone or with his friends at dinners or dancing. These were fun outings, which Wolfgang knew because she related them to Adrianna. He realized that this whirlwind courtship was thrilling and fun for his daughter to achieve new social milestones after her sheltered upbringing.

Two weeks before the wedding date, he noticed Julianna began missing meals. She retreated to her bedroom suite with headaches and other maladies. Mildly concerned, Adrianna attributed her ailments to their busy schedules. Adrianna had told him Julianna needed her rest for the six-month honeymoon travel plans, beginning in Africa. Wolfgang acquiesced to the wise counsel of his wife.

One week before the wedding, Wolfgang received a request from his friend, François, in Paris to come and visit. They often conducted business together, with Wolfgang advising on investments. François worked at Interpol. He and his wife were old family friends. Wolfgang agreed to take the morning train and meet for lunch. He planned to stay the night and return to *Zürich* the following day.

The train ride was uneventful. The two men enjoyed their lunch meeting at a charming bistro, where François filled him in on his family changes. Wolfgang listened to his old friend since he was the customer, feeling it was just the distraction needed after weeks of wedding plans. He told Francois he learned the father of the bride's main role revolved around funding. After lunch, they visited François' office to review more business items and sign papers. Wolfgang presented the investment summaries with all the current numbers and projections. He recommended new technology investments his company believed were beneficial to consider.

With business concluded, François shifted in his chair, facing his old friend, whose expression appeared somber. "My friend, you said your daughter is getting married soon. I'm sorry we cannot attend because my wife isn't up for travel." He wiped his glasses with his monogrammed handkerchief. "Wolfgang, do you recall you asked me to check on the background of young Andreas Müller? It took far longer than I intended to respond. I asked my brother, who works in a different department from me, to see what he could find. He uncovered unsettling information on a renowned scam artist."

Wolfgang felt his chest clench. The excellent food he'd consumed soured in his stomach, and time suspended. He tried to school his features while his insides shattered into tiny pieces. The thought that raced across his mind was that this revelation was before the wedding, even though François had no idea that the groom was the object of his request.

François must have noticed a change Wolfgang couldn't mask when he asked, "I'm sorry not to have replied sooner. Let me share the facts.

"Andreas Müller is one of several aliases used by a young man who meets the description. It took extensive man-hours to look through various documents. The young German has a history of targeting young women. He charms them while he gains information on their families. Blackmail seems to be his goal, though his political ties suggest espionage. Scotland Yard and Interpol suspect he is a deep-cover spy for the KGB as his paymaster. Interpol has orders to arrest him on sight. He sells his information to the highest bidder.

"Additionally, he's left a trail of broken-hearted ladies over the last ten years under as many names. Do not trust him with any of your business or family information. Any inroads you can provide Interpol to apprehend him is appreciated. I'm willing to act as your mediator to Interpol."

Ever one to keep his thoughts close to his chest, Wolfgang calmly replied, "You are certain? Do you have any photographs of this man I can verify? I've had him to dinner several times but didn't consider him a threat to my business."

"Yes, I do have a couple of photographs. People with Polaroid cameras are sending Interpol casual photos, proving amazingly useful. Files are expanding to support many requests with everyday pictures potentially aiding crime-fighting in the future. I'd enjoy discussing the possibilities with you sometime."

Wolfgang nodded in agreement. He looked at the photos of Andreas with one smiling young lady after another by his side, characterizing him as a monster like Dorian Grey incarnate. His heart sank to his stomach, hating what he must tell his daughter. He was too embarrassed to share the details with his client. Graphical information would become a valid resource for law enforcement. For a moment, he was grateful that criminals like Andreas had no idea how changing technology would ensnare them.

"Thank you, my friend, for getting me the information. I must see if I can get the last train home tonight."

"We need to get together more often. The meal was superb, wasn't it."

"It was François. I'll make the investment changes we discussed and send you any other relevant details."

Wolfgang was surprised when he arrived home to find Adrianna waiting for him in the sitting room of their bedroom. Before he could relate the sad news, Adrianna sobbed into his arms.

Composing herself, she moaned. "Julianna is pregnant. She was bereft when she admitted the truth I'd begun to suspect. She fears she'd disappointed us by not waiting until the wedding, but her child would have an honorable name. I tried to reassure her that everything would work out and that you would understand the throes of passion. Their wedding was in less than a week. That reminder made her cry harder."

Wolfgang switched from enraged to gut-punched at the unfairness of everything since Andreas crossed their path. He blamed himself for not doing better for his only child. Not wanting to add to her misery, he didn't share his news from François. "Is something wrong with the wedding? Is she no longer in love with him?" He grasped her hand in his as she teared up.

"Julianna wept as she explained what happened when she told him she was pregnant. He laughed at her foolishness and brushed her aside, saying he had no intention of marrying her. The ring was plaster, and she was a stupid woman." Adrianna wiped her eyes and gripped his hand tighter. "I pressed her for more details. She revealed he'd demanded some confidential bank information more than once. Julianna refused to give in to his request, laughing it off, saying she was too low on the totem pole to know anything important. Honey, she's foolish about him but never about the family business. She confronted him with his responsibility. He threatened her with scandal. He vowed to spread all the sordid details on the society pages unless she gave him the requested information within three days."

Anger consumed Wolfgang, like a wildfire destroying a forgotten forest, especially for not voicing his early concerns. Even in these modern times, such scarlet branding would be impossible to overcome. His daughter was loyal to her core. Trying to determine the best course of action, he paced the room for several minutes. He paused and recanted what François had uncovered on Andreas' background. He wanted his hands around the man's throat and knew he'd feel no remorse if he delivered the charlatan his last breath. A plan of sorts started to take shape in his mind.

"Julianna," he loudly called, "can you come to our room, please?"

His chest tightened when he noticed her red-rimmed eyes and the resignation in her stance. Recalling this and the hours of discussion still caused Wolfgang heartache. Their lives crumbled like a forgotten wedding cake. He held his wife and daughter, trying to stay strong. When they broke apart and sat, he listened to her resolve.

"Mother, Father, I understand the importance of our family business. I know that our friends, no matter how loyal, will shun us because of my foolishness. No one will want to marry me as a soiled woman with an illegitimate child.

Please, promise you'll never tell anyone about this. I will raise and protect my child from my sins." She inhaled deeply and raised her jaw in determination. "I will leave the country before Andreas can ruin our family." She dabbed her eyes with her soggy hankie.

Wolfgang raised an arm over her shoulders and tugged her close. "I understand and respect your thoughts. I can't bear the thought of you being alone without your family close." He deeply breathed and asked, "Would you like to get him behind bars?"

She looked at him with red-rimmed eyes. "How?"

He explained to them both details of what François had uncovered and how he might be able to capture and convict the man who hurt so many young women. He said he thought the authorities could be discreet as he outlined his plan."

"We stop him from ever hurting anyone else? Yes, Father, that I will do."

He hugged her close. "Then we'll discuss relocation plans. We'll help you, and we love you. You are my precious daughter, and your child will be loved too."

Over the next two days, they finalized their strategy to deliver Andreas to justice. Wolfgang contacted François, sharing the sad situation. François confirmed that he could arrange for Andreas to be arrested discretely.

Practicing her lines and tonality repeatedly until Wolfgang nodded his approval. Julianna called Andreas from the house the evening before their scheduled sting operation. "Andreas, I have the information you want. I'm ready to meet you at the bank an hour before opening in the morning. I have the key to let you in." She listened. "No one else will be there that early. We could still be married if you want," she sniffled.

The man snorted his response loudly enough for Wolfgang to hear through the phone's earpiece. She stood taller and more confident in herself, verifying the meeting time. Wolfgang was proud she didn't falter when she hung up the call.

Wolfgang, Julianna, and the authorities were in place before the crook arrived. Wolfgang watched from a crack in his office door as Andreas waltzed into the bank with a smug look of victory when Julianna unlocked the door. Methodical, she had Andreas repeat the items he demanded to ensure nothing was accidentally omitted. The documents appeared real as she leafed through them. When she confirmed the last one, his hand whipped out, and he grabbed the stack, shoving them into his briefcase. She turned and walked toward Wolfgang's office. He stepped out to stand by her as the authorities apprehended the fool.

As Andreas was escorted out, he chanted, "Julianna the Fornicatress was nearly useless on a mattress." He spat on the floor.

Wolfgang nearly gagged as he engulfed his daughter in a hug.
A handful of early-arriving employees heard the ravings but
ignored the situation when they spotted Wolfgang. They went
about their morning chores before opening the bank. Julianna
held her head high as she left the bank, knowing she'd never
work there again. She needed to make a future for herself and
her child where she could start over smarter than before.

At the evening meal, her tears were dried as Julianna outlined
her plans to leave *Zürich* and go to the United States to have
her baby. She explained that when Andreas initially rejected
her, she contacted two of her friends from university who had
moved to New York City. They both worked for Bell Labs and
were learning programming for communications. Julianna
asked about potential openings, wanting to take advantage
of the computer knowledge she recently learned at the bank.
They called back and assured her of a position on the team,
offering her a place to stay while she settled.

Wolfgang felt brokenhearted and watched Adrianna pale as if
stuck by a sudden illness at the idea of her daughter going to
a foreign country alone. An argument ensued. The result was
Adrianna insisted she go with her Julianna. She reminded
Wolfgang that she was an accomplished bank programmer
versed in the current best practices. With her help, Julianna
could get established faster. After Julianna was settled and the
baby was born, Adrianna would return.

It was this decision that haunted Wolfgang. He wanted to go
along, but Adrianna insisted he needed to mind their European

business. His responsibility was to keep it thriving for the family, including Julianna and her child. Several days later, they said goodbye for the first of many times to follow over the years.

The only good note in his memory was the pissant of a man, Andreas ingesting a cyanide capsule while in custody. It occurred the day Julianna and Adrianna departed for New York. In the end, Andreas wasn't man enough to undergo a rigorous interrogation for his mistakes.

Finished arguing with the painful memories, Wolfgang went to his bedroom to write in his journals until sunrise. He agonized over what, if anything, to tell Jacob about his father. Julianna was dead, killed by a reckless driver. She hadn't wanted her child to know and Jacob was his future. He knew one can't break promises even to the dead. Sharing this secret might impact his recently found relationship with his grandson. Secrets like this make you feel ancient. He knew he was old. As he sat with his head in his hands, Wolfgang wished sleep would come so he could dream back his life. When Wolfgang envisioned Jacob, he knew the future was possible, but the past couldn't change. He would love the boy-turned-man until his last breath.

Caribbean Dream

*F*lashes of lightening crackled and the small, seedy bungalow rocked and shuddered from the storm's violent winds. Heavy, moist air entered when Judith rushed through the door, slammed it shut, and engaged the bolt. "Zee," she shouted, "bring me the big towel. I'm dripping everywhere."

Her roommate, Xiamara, or Zee as she preferred, handed the thickest terrycloth towel to Judith.

Judith vigorously rubbed herself head to toe with the towel and said, "I'm sick and tired of this lifestyle, Zee. I work my butt off for chump change." She pulled a glob of soggy bills from her pocket and thrust it at her friend. "Here, put this away."

"What's wrong? Did you have a bad day?" Zee asked.

Briskly rubbing her hair with the towel again, scattering thousands of droplets, Judith grumbled, "We don't have time for fun. I'm as worn out as you are, Zee. Jutting her hip to one side and pointing a thumb toward her chest, she said, "I told another cutie *no thanks* to dinner and a movie," jutting her hop to one side and pointing her thumb toward her chest, "'cause I work the opening shift. I'll grab four hours of sleep tops. Two more days before we get a day of rest."

Zee carefully unfolded the wad. "What's with all the pennies?"

Judith smirked and tossed the towel at her friend. "It's for a table dance, whaddya think?"

Zee retrieved the object with her thumb and index finger and extended it toward her roommate. "Your lingering odor smells like soggy old socks. You might want to shower first. You'll rest better, too."

"Fine, fine, fine!" Judith snatched the wet towel and entered the bathroom, sliding the moving pocket door into place. Undressing herself, she overheard Zee loudly count her night's tips and mumble, "I'll bank this tomorrow." Then, her friend's voice became barely audible. "You're right. Something has to give. I'll find a solution."

Three days later, the two girls stepped out of their cottage and inhaled. Bright sunlight reflected off the water, while gentle breezes carried the light soothing scents of the ocean—the start of a perfect new day. Zee slipped the blindfold over Judith's eyes and carefully secured it around the white-blonde hair. "There." She took her roommate's elbow, guiding her down the long stretch of white sand.

"Zee," she whined "can't you tell me why this is so important that I needed to get up early on my only day off? I'm not too fond of blindfolds too, especially when I'd be happier burying my face in my pillow. I feel like I did when you hosted my twenty-first birthday party. You made me play pin the umbrella on the mojito that I didn't want to drink. Is this adventure going to end like that?"

Undeterred, Zee bubbled, "Jude, you'll love this, trust me. I'm glad we decided to be roomies. We have fun despite working hard, but school is our end goal. I daydream about all the things we'll do after we graduate." She bounced with dance-like steps, tousling her curly copper-brunette hair, tugging Judith by the hand down the beach's packed sand. They hummed a favorite tune and laughed together as they dodged random plants in the sand or rocks.

"Slow down. I can't see where I'm going."

"Keep that blindfold on, Jude, or I'll clip your beautiful hair while you're asleep. Relax. Feel the gentle warmth of the winter sun. Listen to the lapping waves. Inhale that fragrant salty air of the breezes that makes life so special here on San Juan..."

"You takin' me somewhere or writing a travel brochure?"

Zee stopped and whipped off the blindfold. "TADA!" She bowed, then extended her arms and fingertips, "And for only three-quarters of our savings, I present."

Judith's blinking her eyes as if to focus followed the direction of her friend's spread hands. "Ah...what is that? A boat?" A dark cloud covered them briefly as the breeze increased. Judith's eyes narrowed at the weathered beached craft, and she stood as if stunned for several moments in the shadow of the cloud. She rubbed her eyes, and her face turned crimson as she stomped. "Zee," twisting her head, "tell me you didn't buy this almost boat with our tuition fund! No, strike that," she emphasized, shaking her head. "Tell me why you got fleeced out of our university monies."

Zee cringed almost scared as her roommate fisted her hands at her sides. "But, Jude, listen…."

Her friend raised her hand shaking her index finger, eyes ablaze. "We agreed to pool our earnings to return to school this fall. The chump change we make allows us a one-bedroom flat, where we sleep on cots, and almost two square meals a day. We're scrimping enough to pay the tuition fees for those computer classes to better ourselves."

"I know, but if…."

"What is it with you?" Judith railed. "You enjoy our day and night jobs as booth babes and checkout chicks so much that you've sentenced both of us to a third job? Really?"

Xiamara felt crushed as she watched her best friend's eyes fill with tears.

The blond hair lifted in the breeze as she wiped the moisture. "Our degrees promise high-paying tech jobs. You didn't think of our future?"

Zee frowned, disappointed that her friend didn't understand the opportunity this provided. She needed to capture her friend's excitement to unwrap the possibilities. "You miss the point, Judy. We can use this boat to take tourists from the cruise ships' daily dockings out snorkeling. We know the entire San Juan shoreline, with those special hidden places you found. I thought we'd advertise a modest touring service run by two geeky computer nerds trying to earn tuition. People love helping, especially for a cause like education."

Judith gave a nasty scowl. "Zee, don't call me Judy. You know better. I've hated that name since my mom's live-in, or whatever he was, called me that." Judith fanned her hands, encompassing the beached craft. "I told you when we moved in I wanted more. The tuition money was our ticket out of poverty. Heck, having a single bank account saves us on bank fees. You threw away savings that took us months to scrape together—geez. We shoulda talked first."

She turned away and shot a fist to the sky, shook it, and took a breath as she turned back. "Please, tell me you at least got some magic beans to go with this deal. Maybe we'll bump into Jack and climb the beanstalk to find our degrees."

Zee felt she needed to explain and opened her mouth, but Judith sarcastically continued, "Exactly how did you think we'd get this boat from here to anywhere without an engine? Who were you thinking would row this tub full of passengers, gear, and refreshments to our target destinations? Wouldn't one of us have to steer? Argh!" she added, stomping her feet like a three-year-old.

Tired of the tirade, Zee took a step making them nose-to-nose. "Boy, you got your panties in a wad. How about letting me finish? You don't see the sailing mast and jib also part of the deal. Ronaldo agreed to use his labor to add the rigging to our private tour craft." She jabbed an index finger on her buddy's chest. "So, STOP calling it a boat."

Zee inhaled and closed her eyes, thinking of the idealistic thoughts that had her initially agreeing to the deal to acquire the boat. "We use our natural, free wind supply to sail tourists to rarely visited destinations on this island. We have zero competition that focuses on the shoreline from the sea." Setting her jaw, she added a grin and a friendly pat on the shoulder. "Then we anchor in some nice coves so our guests can snorkel. I've got a line on some used gear, too. Honest," she did a quick cross-heart motion, "I know we can do this."

The corners of Judith's mouth tilted upward, followed by a gentle head shake. Zee hoped she had broken through the anger and opened her friend's mind to the opportunities ahead. Then Judith closed her eyes while tears streamed down her cheeks, alarming Zee.

"Ah, don't cry."

Judith's forearm banished the waterworks and stuttered, "Sailing? We know nothing about boats." She took a deep breath. "We have challenges making the double mocha lattés infused with dandelion extract at the Coffee Shack, where we at least get tips. Now you're talking about sailing a barely serviceable boat with some bolt-on parts?"

Zee sensed a shift in her buddy's tone and grinned. "I thought about that. I found some free how-to-sail-your-boat videos on YouTube. This cute hunk shows how to tack into the wind, use the jib sail, and steer. We can both watch and take turns practicing."

Judith closed her eyes again and released a long breath. "Okay, Miss I-Thought-It-All-Out, how do we snag tourists? Do you think we can persuade them to spend money with us? When you convince me that's solved, we can bring them to our *Lily of San Juan,* where we sail them to the first cove with some fish to watch."

"I like the name—good one. I've already gotten permission to use the school printers and computers to make up some snappy brochures. We'll use these to hustle the local hotel concierges and businesses to steer people our way. We can also stand at the disembarkation ramps and hawk our wares."

"How is it possible that your harebrained scheme is starting to sound good?" A grin barely suppressed as she added, "We need to hype the fact that we're putting ourselves through school. It's like a crowdfunding exercise for the day-trippers. They can pat themselves on the back for paying more for the underdogs than the bigger services." With a smirk, she said. "We, of course, encourage tipping. And you can get your angelic smile on."

Zee cleared her throat and clapped. "Good one. Since we're planning some uniqueness, how about digging out your cute bikini? Isn't the color close to …, your *Lily of San Juan after a new coat of paint*?" Mischievously grinning and gesturing to their new venture. "You still have it, right?"

She snorted. "Yeah, you mean the one that's a bit too tight in the boobs?"

"Yep, the one that makes guys trip all over themselves to get your attention. We both know I can't pull that off with my pear shape."

"Are you saying I get to be the lead diver, too? Won't it be a bit too revealing? We don't want to offend wives or dates."

"I don't think it's immodest, just provocative," Zee insisted. "We'll add an elegant cover-up that doesn't hide totally to convince some male patrons to add to their tip. I mean, come on, Jude. Your long blonde mane and ideal body make you a natural point person. I have the friendly smile and great chestnut curls but am far more suited to heavy lifting."

"You always make me feel special," Judith said, slightly hugging Zee. "I tend to hide beneath a shapeless dress except at work. I was annoyed 'til you consoled me when my boss insisted on fitted uniforms. You're my oldest friend. I don't see the chunky, plain girl you do. All I ever see is a person with a heart of gold and my best friend." Her hand reached toward the cinnamon-colored ringlets "And, gad, I wish I had those curls in my hair."

Judith exhaled sharply, shrugged, then unexpectedly scolded, "You could have discussed this with me before raiding our funds. It hurts thinking that you're becoming just another person conning me. Remember how we met? Two loners at lunch. Everyone we trusted stole money, food, or clothes from us and then vanished. I never thought you'd do that to me, Zee."

"I'm sorry. I was trying to help get us ahead faster. I should have talked with you beforehand. But I didn't run. I'm still here—for us." Zee grimaced. "You were working a double shift. The bartender, Ronaldo, needed the funds badly. I refused to get sucked into lending him a penny." Zee gestured with a sweep of her arm. "So, he sold us his pride and joy."

With a resigned look, Judith nodded. "Okay, I see what you were thinking. We were top of our class in our first year of junior college. Tell me, can we make a profit with *Lily*?"

"You'll be glad to know I negotiated four months of free dock space while our business ramps." Zee pulled out her notebook and moved to share the contents. "Then, I found this helpful person at the Chamber of Commerce who gave me their research figures on the island's tourist trade for the last several years. If we can capture a modest seven percent of this business with lower prices and more personalization, we should return our investment and triple our tuition savings in seven months."

Zee noted the glint in her buddy's eye because they'd always connected on numbers.

"Even if we capture four percent, Zee, we can make the tuition." She rubbed her palms together. "What's next?"

"Now we just need a catchy name for the business to get the advertising started."

Appearing to get into the project's spirit, Judith giggled after tapping her chin for a few beats. "Try this, Zee. We call it *Fall Diving Bits* since we're hustling our fall tuition. I'll be the *Head Diving Bits,* and you're the *Sailor Diving Bits.* Your idea of a crowdfunding exercise with goals that continue to expand with each successful increment is brilliant."

Zee offered a high-five and hip bump as her excitement rose, and she squealed with glee. "I like The Diving Bits better as we might want to keep it going between semesters."

"Alight. That works."

"Jude, we work through those sailing tutorials after our shift tonight. The high tide here in San Juan is on its way, so I'll phone Ronaldo to help me get the Lily of San Juan into her berth to prepare for her maiden cruise." Inclining her head to the approaching strangers, Zee added. "Can you work your magic charms with those guys walking this way to help push *Lily* into the water? The dock is only half a mile up the shoreline."

Judith immediately transformed into character, tossed her hair back over her shoulder, and tied her dress around the waist, exposing her stomach and short shorts with shapely legs that met at her curved bottom. "Like this?"

"Uh, let's not overdo it. Wow, those are tight short shorts, but you look great. I know you don't want charm on display that promises too much collateral in return. Lower the tie-up just a bit."

Judith chuckled. "Point taken." She motioned to the three guys on the beach, who happily accommodated the two smiling flirts.

The girls spent every extra moment outfitting the *Lily of San Juan for the remainder of the month.* Both girls daydreamed of non-stop business when the mast and sail were mounted. A fresh, glossy coat of turquoise paint adorned the hull. The craft's name in white script gained oohs and aahs from other boat owners and the marina regulars.

They were nearly ready for the cruise ship docking next Sunday. The photo at the top of *Lily of San Juan* made a difference in the brochures. Positive comments, distribution permission from several businesses, and a few contributions to their college funds boosted their confidence.

Judith marked their completion with a happy face on the calendar in the bungalow after they diligently practiced their YouTube training, with mixed results. By the end of day twenty, they were sore but competent sailors. The breezes on this side of the island were ideal for practicing. They scouted the deep enough coves with minimal surf to allow them easy maneuvering. They rehearsed securing their position with an anchor and then releasing it until the process became flawless.

Judith was surprised when the successful support from the small businesses failed to extend to the tour brokers. For them to promote to the shipping lines, they required positive reviews. Consequently, when the first ship docked, and passengers exited, the girls acted like carnival barkers to get attention. Finally, after Judith's umpteenth ten-second elevator pitch, they snagged a single older gentleman.

"Ladies," John Maling said, "show me your boat and perhaps a pretty beach where I can take some photos of the shoreline. My prior visits were spent in town."

Zee pulled Judith aside and whispered, "Is he okay? He's not a letch?"

"Nay, he's all right. Besides, we can take him. Don't worry. Let's be polite."

Turning toward their first customer. "John," she exclaimed, "I'm Xiamara, Zee for short; we're glad you decided to sail with us. But don't try anything funny. We know how to fight!"

John laughed uproariously for nearly a minute until they finally joined in.

"You two are a hoot," he jested. "No funny stuff, I assure you. You're too young for me, but your spiel was good. Show me the secret cove, ladies."

Judith held out her hand. "I'm Captain Judith, John." As they reached the boat, she handed him a life vest off the rack next to the dock and motioned. "Welcome aboard."

Judith hopped onboard after him while Zee secured the ropes. They snapped on their vests as they sat. Using the oars, they maneuvered *Lily* out of the slip. Away from the other crafts, Zee unfurled the sail. They caught a nice breeze that propelled them toward their destination.

John pitched in to help as the wind shifted. "If you lean slightly in the direction you're headed, it'll help your rudder get a better turn ratio."

Zee applied his suggestion. "You're right. Thanks, John."

Anchoring at the cove worked after the second try. John again made recommendations that proved spot on. "I work most of the islands in the Caribbean, setting up wind power for local governments. This region has been plagued with fierce storms forever, so harnessing the wind appeals to the communities. That part of your pitch convinced me to try this little outing."

"Thank you. Zee had the original idea with the sailing aspect. I'm glad she was right. Do you think we have a chance to gain more customers? The ship tour brokers want references."

John smiled like an indulging father. "Neither of you seem afraid of hard work. A little more practice and your steering will get smoother, Zee. The spots you've shown me are good. They aren't easy hikes nor part of the cruise line's sailing courses. Let's try some snorkeling!"

Judith became the instructor and showed John how to put on his gear. She guided him to her previously scouted rock formations below the surface. John was delighted with the marine life that darted in and around the coral. He helped Judith get back on board.

Zee broke out the snacks and sodas. They laughed at John's jokes. The girls explained a bit more about their school plans then headed back to the docking point. John exited the boat, saluted the two girls, and paid them.

"John, you made this trip a lot of fun. Thank you," Judith said with a grin.

"Come back soon, John," Zee added.

"Don't worry about that. I'll give your information to several tour brokers I know. Your business will increase." Then he added with a grin. "Was I a good first customer?"

The girls chorused, "Yes."

He laughed. "You'll do all right. See ya in a couple of weeks. I'll call the number on your card and leave a message about my next arrival date. Take care. And, next time, have a little beer, wine, and rum for your guests. I like red, myself."

As they cleaned up the boat and stowed their gear, they talked about making the trips more enjoyable. John had suggested they announce landmarks for the tourists as a high runner and Judith should add her enthusiasm to any points of interest. Zee mentioned practicing additional sailing during her spare time. They picked up a tour a day over the next week. Each trip improved, but they liked taking out couples, so they focused on those targets. Their positive ratings increased on the website Zee built.

Good to his word, John provided recommendations, and word of mouth positively impacted their business. They added multiple daily tours to meet the morning and afternoon demands when a ship docked. Some days, depending upon the docking and departure times, three tours for two and one-half hours each became doable. Scheduling precision and ratings for the small enterprise steadily improved. The tour income continued to grow but didn't match their day jobs wages as cashiers. Even though the sailing was more taxing, they decided to focus on excursions during daylight hours and keep their waitressing jobs at night. The bar work tips added a needed income cushion at this point.

Sadly, their success was noticed by local riffraff, who offered island services during tourist season to larger tourist parties. The Diving Bits became the target of another snorkeling tour operator, Benjy. Disheveled and arrogant, he swaggered toward their boat's berth one morning before the ship-of-the-day docked. He kicked their cleaning rags and the bucket into the water as he closed the distance to *Lily's* berth. "You girls are crowding my space," he spat. "Stay outta my swim lane. But find something else to do besides crowding my snorkeling gig here on the island."

Intimidated by the gruff overweight operator with his oily complexion and tobacco brown teeth, Judith watched Zee turn pasty before she appeared to melt into the furthest corner of the boat as if to disappear.

Judith looked up with false bravado and confidently countered without a second thought, "Are you here to buy us out?"

Benjy shook his head dismissively as he extracted a toothpick from his mouth and snorted, "Nice try, sweet chops. Why pay for something I can run out of business? You ain't got the proper tour operator sticker displayed. I'll turn you in and let Shore Patrol do the unpleasantries of confiscating your joke of a boat." He walked away, guffawing as he called over his shoulder. "See ya 'round, bitches."

Judith jumped up on the dock and waved her fist in the air. "That's THE Diving Bits to you, Benjy," she shouted in her deepest voice. "Don't underestimate us."

Benjy kept maniacally laughing while he walked away without a glance back.

Judith turned back to the boat to see the pained expression on Zee's face. "Don't you dare cry over this, Zee! Who the hell does Doctor Grimy think he's dealing with? You stay here and get us ready for our next group. I'm gonna fix this and get the proper paperwork." Judith watched Zee swipe at a few stray tears, hoping her friend would pull it together. "You good, Zee?"

Zee nodded. "I can get everything ready before sundown if he doesn't return. You go on. I'm fine."

"He won't return today, but I'll be back," Judith replied. She turned and stormed off like one of Poseidon's daughters, hunting for the mortal who hurt her pet fish. Everyone on the dock could hear Judith's favorite colloquial phrases used to reflect on someone's ancestry uttered loudly coupled with highly animated gestures echoing in her wake.

A while later, Judith startled Zee as she jumped on the boat and handed over a thick packet.

"Judith," Zee squeaked, "you scared me. What's this?"

"Open it."

Zee carefully opened the packet; her eyes grew big as she thumbed through the contents. "How did you get these boat and snorkeling operator licenses? These normally take weeks, but you've only been gone a few hours."

Judith smirked. "Let's just say the Shore Marshal is fully on board with us being tour operators and promises to look into Doctor Grimy and his threatening statements."

"These aren't cheap, Jude. I know because I priced them when planning our adventure. That's why I didn't bother pursuing them. It wasn't anywhere in our budget. I figured we'd be too small to mess with." Then Zee demanded, "You didn't promise him the *Pooty,* did you?"

Highly annoyed, Judith felt her anger rise at Zee's accusation and delivered an *are you kidding me look* before she replied.

"No, I didn't promise him the *Pooty*. I called our favorite gentleman, John. I asked if he could use his wit and gender to persuade the issuing official to grant us a temporary license. We're on the hook to make good. Then John promised he'd extend it at the end of the season for next year, provided we show our tuition receipts." She stuck out her tongue and added, "Satisfied?"

"Why would John do a favor like that? What do we owe him, or shouldn't I ask?"

"What's with you? Favors don't require horizontal exchange unless you want that." Judith felt exasperated. "Remember the first trip where John over-tipped us when he provided his phone number and offered to fund our tour operation? He also plainly stated there were no strings attached. I wanted us to make this work independently, but I appreciated his promise to tell folks we were a fun tour. You may recall, he said our cause had merit."

"Are you saying he's wealthy? I thought he earned a good living, but I didn't expect this." She sniffled. "It's so generous."

"Duh. He gave us a great tip on the second trip," Judith emphasized. "No matter. When I called and explained the situation, he chuckled. You know he told us he has connections in the Caribbean. He'll be here again next week and prebooked for our three tours that day. He wants to have some relaxation with intelligent, determined ladies taking him out on snorkeling adventures when he's in port."

"Okay, it'll be his third trip. We can take him to that new spot we found," Zee added.

"He mentioned the wine again for the return trip to shore. The Boones Farm lacked something he preferred, so he said he'd arrange wine delivery before we set sail again. I guess he's a wine connoisseur. Who knew?"

Zee appeared dumbfounded. "He's wealthy, connected, and kind. I'm sorry I was so suspicious. I take it John leaned on the issuing official. Nice one." She raised a hand to fist bump. "I'm not used to people offering to help for nothing. However, as a point of honor, we must pay him back at the end of the season."

"Agreed."

The sun reflected off rippled water, playfully dancing with the wind. Zee sang a silly pop song while Judith added the final supplies for their day's first tour. They spotted the cruise ship easing toward the pier, suggesting another hour before tourists touched the ground. Judith was cleaning the snorkels and masks when Zee stopped her song mid-line.

Judith looked toward her friend, who visibly shook and stepped back slightly. Following the direction of Zee's gaze, she spotted an older pontoon boat with a faded canopy, motored to dock near *Lily of San Juan*. Not taking her eyes off the muscular guys, she blocked Zee from their line of sight.

Zee's voice caught in her throat as she softly growled, "I've seen them before, Jude, but never spoke. I recognize them from Benjy's outfit. I'm scared. They can't bring good news or want a social call."

Zee cautiously stooped, snagging both their sailor's bludgeon sticks, and handed one to Judith. They whopped loudly as each girl slapped them against their hands. Their eyes focused on the two men while they maneuvered their boat close to *Lily's* berth.

The rugged guys looked at one another, the ladies, and then back again. They smiled in unison and raised their hands.

Standing tall like a warrior princess, Judith challenged, "Hold it right there. You both work for Benjy. Last time he swaggered by, he threatened to run us out of business." Her eyes shifted momentarily to Zee, who raised her chin.

Zee rose and asked, "What's your business?"

The taller, lanky man grinned at his buddy and directed his comment to the blond. "Ah, the rumors are true. He threatened to reduce the competition. Good call, Matias, we were right to quit that jerk-weed."

Matias smiled broadly and splayed his arms, his hands facing down. "We don't work for him anymore. Can we talk to you? Please."

Judith studied the two men, noting they were roughly the same age and appeared fit. Matias had some extra meat around the middle. "Sure, but I'd rather you stay away from our boat. What's up?"

Judith frowned when she felt Adolfo's eyes checking her out from head to toe and back.

He raised an eyebrow and added a smile. "Sorry, ma'am. We're here to ask for a spot with your group. I can't help but admit I appreciate the scenery. Benjy is less than worthless. He owes us a couple of weeks of wages."

Matias glanced toward the brunette and added with a grin. "This here's our boat, free and clear. We work hard, and we like people. Plus, me and Adolfo know the waters around here."

Zee wiggled her fingers in hello. "My name is Xiamara, but you can call me Zee. She's Judith. I've seen you both around. Glad you aren't associated with Benjy now."

Adolfo set his jaw. "You ever hear the saying, keep your enemies closer? We hung close, but he cheated us. He's also a backstabber, so we came here. We'll watch your back and handle any overflow business from larger groups. You ladies have a good rep growing with the brokers, whereas Benjy's is dwindling."

"Guys, nice as extra support would be, we're on a shoestring budget. We can't pay for employees, even if they come with a boat," Judith said.

"What if we partnered and split our earnings with Adolfo and the cute one for what they contribute?" exclaimed Zee. "Their boat IS larger than ours. Together, we could cater to larger groups."

Blushing from his neck up, Matias stammered, "What's the name of your business, Curls?"

Zee blushed at her outburst and giggled. "Judith is the Head Diving Bits, and I'm the Sailing Diving Bits. But Curls works, too."

They chortled, and Judith observed the guys visibly relaxed.

Adolfo recounted, "We've worked for Benjy for months but got paid piecemeal. We got the leftover food and drinks from the tours, usually meager. We do get direct tips from the customers, but we split them. We heard about you two around town. People say you want to return to the tech school, and we think that's cool. Then Benjy bragged he'd run you girls out of business."

Matias nodded in agreement. "We don't want to work for that dump truck no more. Yesterday, we quit. We want to compete fairly and honestly because that's who we are. Let's work together, ladies."

"Uh, work for a dump truck?" questioned Judith.

"Yeah, Benjy, the dump truck. Always dumping on someone: his employees, competitors, the cruise lines, or the suppliers.

Never said he's to blame. We don't want to catch his mental disease of being Teflon, so we came to you two. We heard your customers like you, and they recommend you. You also laugh and cut up. You treat folks nice," Matias said.

"Zee and I need to meet our guests at the pier in a few minutes. We'll talk about your offer and weigh our options. Let's get back together early in the morning at the coffee shop to discuss."

Adolfo nodded. "Thank you, both. We'll see you tomorrow around 6:30."

The guys drifted back to their boat. They sat on their deck chatting.

Judith thumbed her fingers and picked at her nails, worried that they might be waiting for an opportunity to damage their boat while she and Zee were getting their passengers.

"Zee, you stay here while I go greet our guests. If anything happens, yell for the guard on duty. As I walk by the gate, I'll ask him to keep an ear out."

Zee grinned. "Okay, I'll watch him, I mean them, like a hawk. I'm not worried in the least, though." She touched Judith's elbow, indicating she had more to say. "We could split our daily take in half because they'll be hauling more paying customers than us." Then Zee tilted her head to one side and started to gnaw her thumbnail. "It would be fairer if we split by the passengers per boat and activities."

Annoyed, Judith gazed at her friend. "There you go again with your do-gooder streak." She grinned. "But yeah, you're right. Let's talk later about it. I don't want these folks to wait."

Judith jumped slightly when Adolfo unexpectedly spoke right behind her. "Before you go, let's approach this differently. Our boat is motorized, but yours is a sailing vessel with more panache. We would charge less per person for the motorized transport with the scruffy males. Folks can sail with the two mermaids for a few extra shekels. Maybe we offer pictures of the two of you with them as souvenirs. No one would pay for pictures with us unless we dressed up like Jack Sparrow, but I see good revenue with you two."

Zee blushed from toe to forehead. "Uh, no one would want to pay for pictures with me. I'm not…."

Judith glared at her friend, then turned on the two guys and pointed them toward their boat. "Timeout, all of you. You guys get back to your boat. I need to grab our guests. Zee, watch our stuff."

Zee saluted, chuckled, and sent a wink toward the guys.

Judith muttered, "Geez. Drama. I so don't like drama."

The guys jumped into their boat. She could feel them watching her she stepped on the dock and stomped off at a good clip. She knew Zee would be chatting it up with the boys before she returned. Quickly locating their reservation guests waving their tickets in hand, Judith was confused to see them surrounded by five others.

"Mr. and Mrs. Marson, I'm Judith with The Diving Bits. Are you ready?"

Grinning lovebirds, the woman gushed, "Yes, but the guests on either side of our cabin would like to come along. I know there weren't more tickets, but we thought we'd ask."

Dumbfounded, Judith looked up at the clouds and offered a small prayer. Pasting on a big smile, she looked at the excited tourists. "We can make this work, I think," she grinned. "But I need to collect your tour funds in advance. Since we're not on the ship favorites, I have no way to auto-charge your cabin. We can do cash or Zella. There's an ATM on the way to the dock if that's easier."

A cheer erupted from the group.

Mr. Marson added, "Thank you so much. We'll pay for double your tour fee for helping us out." Marson quickly peeled off the cash and handed it to Judith.

They headed toward the marina. Judith mentally calculated the additional life vests and food needed. She breathed a sigh of relief that the other vessel was in place when they arrived.

The looks of surprise from everyone in the boats shifted to smiles and greetings while they listened to Mr. Marson explain the situation. Judith grinned and motioned to Adolfo. Handing him cash, she listed out what he needed to retrieve.

Zee smiled as she announced, "Great, I am Zee, the sailing lead. You have already met Judith. We'll lead the way to the first cove. Mr. and Mrs. Marson, you're with us in *Lily of San Juan,* and the rest of you'll be with Matias."

Matias added, "Join me on the *Mini Black Pearl*, mates. My partner Adolfo will return shortly with our provisions and safety gear. Find your spots. We're set to sail when everything is stowed."

Adolfo returned less than half an hour later, pulling a wagon with vests and provisions. Adolfo tied the wagon to the edge of their berth when everything was stowed.

Judith cleared her throat to get the guests' attention while Zee and Matias handed out vests. Adolfo remained next to her on the dock. Happy faces centered her in her teal bikini with her bronze-tanned figure, demonstrating the proper use of life vests. Adolfo joined the conversation to explain water safety and reminded everyone to stay seated while the boat moved. After delivering the safety message, Zee led *Lily of San Juan* out of the harbor with Matias following with the *Mini Black Pearl*.

San Juan's beauty and the weather matched the cruise ship's advertising. The warm sun kissed the island guests as breezes scented by the salty seas wrapped them into soft hugs. Their tourists delighted with the sights and snacked when the boats docked side by side after the snorkeling adventure. Photos featuring the girls from The Diving Bits were a hit, as predicted by the guys. Sighs of regret sounded when the boats returned to the dock. The Marson party waved farewell with huge smiles and handed Judith extra tips. Matias and Adolfo helped the girls clean all the gear and return the rented equipment. Judith suggested they head to dinner and discuss future possibilities.

After sunset graced the shoreline with vibrant oranges, reds, and golds, the four ended up at a patio table at the bistro where both girls worked as servers, though they had no shift tonight. They enjoyed their burgers, fries, and drinks.

"I want to know which of you two subscribed to the crystal ball," joked Judith. "We'd have missed that revenue if you hadn't shown up." She handed out funds to each man after deducting the cost of the supplies.

"This is a fair split based on the passengers you hauled," Zee added. "As you kindly suggested, we took a premium for those who snorkeled. Thanks for not being jerks."

Zee slapped hands with Judith. "We did great today, Jude. Together, we can offer up to eight tour tickets adding a premium for snorkeling."

Clicking their glasses in a united cheer. "Prost!"

"Better find your pirate outfit," Judith smirked. "Adolfo, you'd be perfect as the bearded Jack Sparrow."

Adolfo interjected with a gleam in his eye. "Does this mean…?"

Zee excitedly interrupted, "We'll draw up a contract tonight that you can sign tomorrow. You're going to help advertise our exclusive outings."

Judith rolled her eyes.

Matias said, "Let's do a picture to mark this occasion, Curls."

"All right, group selfie! Group selfie!" Judith touched her hair, scrunching up the sides.

Matias changed the settings on his smartphone and propped it on the tabletop. They closed ranks and grinned as the timer pinged. They repeated the posing for each phone, with Zee sticking her tongue out on the last one at Judith.

After several high-fives with each other and a ceremony handshake agreement, Judith asked, "What's Benjy going to do when he finds out we're working together?"

Adolfo's eyes flashed with anger. "Don't care. We agreed to be partners. We don't go back on our word. We'll protect you."

Judith smiled like a Cheshire Cat. "You two are hereby dubbed *The Diving Bytes* since we're *The Diving Bits*. Let's make customers happy."

The little company of two watercraft with a crew of four took customers snorkeling throughout the spring and well into summer. The team pooled everything, including the tips, and then split it daily to keep the earnings square. It worked for paying as-needed repairs. John Maling made the infrequent trip with the ladies and heartily approved their business expansion. After one trip, John had custom tee shirts sent for everyone.

Judith and Zee were making significant progress toward their tuition goals, with school starting in early October. Adolfo and Matias were thrilled with their earnings. Now and then, they saw Benjy glaring at them as they escorted their day-trippers. They ignored him, even with his annoyingly loud, derogatory comments.

The operation ran smoothly like a Rolex, typically handling two daily trips, sometimes three. The summer season kept the cruise ships docking and a few locals took advantage of party trips on the weekends. Toward the end of summer, the weather grew erratic and unpredictable.

As they outfitted the boats one morning, Adolfo suggested, "You know, Jude, we'll be hit with afternoon swells and rains for the rest of September. We might want to keep to our motorized boat and save Lily of San Juan for the first tour of the morning if the weather looks good."

Judith nodded, but Zee commented, "We spoke of this last night. Remember, we secure the boat before we do any afternoon runs in case the weather shifts."

"The same way we secure her at night," Judith confirmed.

Matias indicated, "I'll be responsible for checking the weather daily to optimize our planning."

Weather forecasting around Puerto Rico is an inexact science. Still, their scheduling helped for several days. The seas were bumpy, but each tour experienced a safe return. Guests on one of the trips said the return was like an unexpected roller-coaster ride.

Then, one morning, things changed when they gathered at the dock.

"We can do the tour today with both boats," Mathias declared, "but we gotta return thirty to forty-five minutes earlier."

Judith nodded and met the eight ticketed guests at the appointed spot. They took the short walk to the local dock area, chattering like kids about to enter a carnival. The group divided between the two boats and sat facing the dock for instructions. When they started with the life vest instruction, Judith thought it a good omen with bright blue skies and whipped cream clouds. "Folks, isn't this a beautiful day?"

Adolfo dressed as the notorious swashbuckler, added his safety speech. "No standing while the boats are moving. During this time of year, the weather rapidly changes. If needed for safety, we may head back early." He bowed and dipped his hat to the ladies with an elegant bow.

Everyone nodded. As the boats departed, they started laughing, taking pictures, and snacking toward the target cove. Two couples added goggles and snorkels then began the exploration below the surface for sea creatures. The other four splashed in the water on rafts secured to the *Mini Black Pearl.* Judith noticed the murky water was the worst she'd seen. Everyone returned to their boats when she told the guests it was time.

One guest pointed toward the west. "Look how black the clouds are getting; boy, they're moving fast."

Matias announced. "Folks, I need you to sit at the boat's bow. Make certain your vests are tight. We will race for the dock behind *Lily of San Juan.*" Then, shouting to Zee, "Are you good, or do you need help? It's going to get rough."

Zee smiled at her guests and swallowed hard. "I got this. Let's go."

Judith spoke evenly, while her insides churned in panic, "The dark storm clouds are coming fast, which means the wind will blow everything. Put your shoes on and hold tight to your bags." Then she placed the back of her hand on her forehead and dramatically implored, "Fasten your vests, folks, it's gonna be a bumpy ride."

She chuckled, and they followed suit. Gusty winds caused increasingly tormented seas. Judith glanced toward Zee, who fought to maintain the most direct course. Judith secured the mainsail's boom and then showed Zee how to reset her hands on the tiller for a better hold. Judith's worries rose, and she chewed her lip. It felt like she was being tested in a closing act between wills and expertise. Passengers held onto one another with flashes of fear displayed in their eyes, and prayers whispered on their lips.

Arriving at the marina without issue, the seafarers secured their respective boats. Guests cheered the landing, and the crews let go sighs of relief. The dock oscillated from the increasingly rough waters as the passengers scrambled for a footing and then rushed toward their cruise ship on the adjoining dock. Judith ensured the guests made it to their gangway, then rushed back to help Zee and the boys finish securing the crafts and supporting gear. Unsecured items from nearby boats picked up by the wind flew across the dock and into the water. Heavy rains assaulted them, and crafts banged into the bumpers of their berths. The warm air made it bearable.

Judith hollered, "Zee, let's finish this and get to cover."

Adolfo and Matias fastened their boat down and took off at a dead run toward the bar for cover from the pounding wind with rain plastering their hair and clothes to their bodies.

Finally, Zee double-checked the last rope and wiped the r ivers of water from her eyes. "Okay," she yelled, "*Lily's* secure! Let's go!"

The storm abated by mid-morning the next day, and the team met at the dock. Slowly, the four walked down the dock lanes, staring in disbelief at the storm's aftermath.

Judith silently prayed that *Lily* was not damaged and held tight to Zee's hand.

Matias lamented, "Wow, what a mess. It'll take weeks to repair this marina. Some boats were tied wrong. These two boats tore through the marina boards like a hot knife through butter. What a shame."

Judith cried, "Oh my, the dock board sliced through that boat's hull. I had no idea the wind was that strong. No wonder John wants to capture it for energy, but it's not easily controlled." Then she stopped, and Zee nearly pulled over her.

Judith watched as Zee rushed to the empty berth and knelt. Judith saw tears run down Zee's cheeks as she inspected the ropes, lax and dangling.

"Jude, I promise I triple-tied these like Matias showed me. I pulled all ways. These were tight when we left. Even in the driving rain, I promise I did it right."

The reality of their loss struck Judith like a punch to the gut. She studied the area in every direction, but there was no sign of their boat.

Then Zee exclaimed, "Look," as she held up one end of the main rope, "Someone cut her ropes. It wasn't my sloppy knots at all. Dammit, *Lily* is probably halfway to Havana by now. And we're out of business."

Adolfo walked back and numbly stated, "Ours too. Gone."

Matias noticed Zee's tears, wrapped his arms around her shoulders, and pulled her close.

Judith ground her teeth. "Were your mooring lines cut as well?" Both men nodded.

Disgusted, Adolfo suggested, "Come on, I've got a pretty good idea where our boats ended up."

They hiked down the shoreline before finding a small salvage party working to restore order to the damaged area. Small boats lined up like sacrificial lambs, claiming to facilitate clean-up. The four of them spotted their two vessels. They spotted Benjy front and center with the local authorities pressing for ownership.

Judith marched up hands on her hips. "Hey, Benjy, you cut the mooring ropes on our boats. I bet you led them just far enough to claim salvage." Louder still, she added, "Is that how you treat everyone who works harder than you do?"

Overhearing the accusation, the shore official looked confused. "These are yours? Can you prove they belong to you? They had no papers on them and no registration plates. Sorry, but according to maritime salvage laws, anyone finding them can claim salvage rights."

Benjy laughed in celebration of his obvious win.

Zee smiled sweetly at the official, handing him papers from her fanny pack. "These are our registration papers, sir." Then, pointing toward *Lily*, she added, "They'll match the plates under those seats."

She snorted at Benjy, "Judith told me you'd try something like this, but I didn't believe you would stoop that low. Still, we removed the registration plates and fastened them into the wood under the left side seats of each boat."

All the color drained from Benjy's face then got replaced with a crimson tone fueled by rage. He sputtered, trying to form a useless protest.

The official ignored Benjy's noise and motioned them toward the two boats. He searched both boats, then returned and handed the papers to Zee. The official grinned as he faced Benjy. "Denied."

It took them several hours to move the boats back to the water and finally get them to their rightful mooring spots at the marina. They were tired but happy with how things had turned out.

Judith and Zee met with Matias and Adolfo at the bar a few days later to celebrate. Adolfo brought the drinks to the table.

Judith started, "To my best friend Zee for a wild plan that worked. We've paid next semester in full." They clinked glasses and sipped. She added, "Here's to comping beers tonight for our new partners."

They toasted and drank again.

Adolfo chimed in. "To our business partners who'll let us buy out their shares in the business."

"Yes," Judith said, smiling. "But only if we can work during class breaks."

Glasses clicked again, and they took generous swallows.

Matias grinned and hugged Zee close. "To some great girls, we consider more than sisters. Congratulations."

They cheered and finished off their beers. Zee asked for another round.

Zee wobbled a bit as she raised her glass toward Judith. "I promise the next wild idea I come up with, I probably won't ask for your permission."

Glaring at Zee for a moment, Judith burst out laughing. "Agreed, if they all turn out this great, why not?"

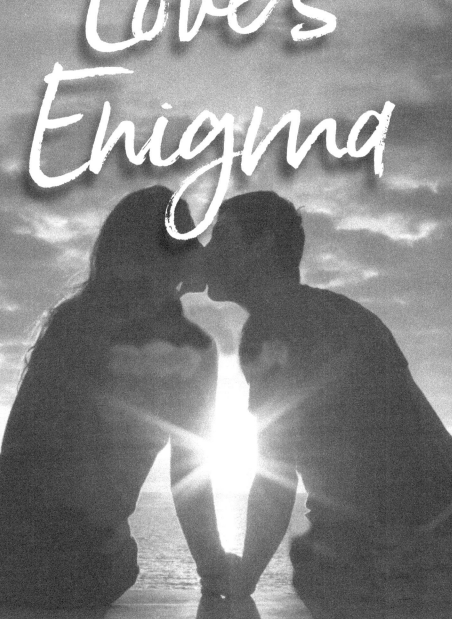

The area Buzz found was semi-deserted, with a few streetlights winking on, signaling early evening. From his work at his father's bank, he thought this area was part of a revitalization effort by the city. They parked in front of the aged Bronx apartment building, its front door ajar.

In the passenger seat of the spacious SUV, Buzz checked the directions on his phone. "This is the place. Let's go, guys."

Undeterred by the eerie quiet of the deteriorated neighborhood and the No-Trespassing signage, Buzz raced up the stoop, their footsteps the only sounds outside of their breathing. Inside, Buzz came to an abrupt halt, causing Jacob and Carlos to nearly collide with him.

"Here!" Buzz lifted his arm, then yelled, "The GPS indicates up these stairs." They each engaged the flashlight feature on their phones.

They rushed the two worn flights, barely noticing the peeling paint in the poorly lit interior of the decrepit apartment building. Buzz led them through the open door, nearly tripping over the two bound, gagged, and unconscious men on his right.

Buzz shifted his focus to the center of the room, brightened by faint light streaming from the curtainless window, and his chest clenched when he saw the chair. He closed the gap, identifying the bloody, battered body of the woman he loved. Taut ropes tied around the torso restrained her in the chair. The mass of tangled dark hair hid her face. Rips and tears in her shirt, especially the sleeves, looked like a consequence of the beating. Her tight skinny jeans intact, suggested she hadn't been violated.

He lifted her chin and brushed matted bloody hair from her face. Ebony-colored eyes fluttered open with a slight sign of recognition before drifting shut. "Zara, can you hear me?" He bent his head and felt her shallow exhale on his ear. He glanced at his friends. "Guys, she's breathing, but I don't see any blood flowing."

Carlos appeared on his left and did a cursory assessment. "Her pulse is shallow. It looks like she's been punched in the face and body, maybe kicked by the guys on the floor."

Jacob said, "Agreed. These two are out but breathing. Their bloodied knuckles are bruised."

"The hell with them," Buzz called over his shoulder angrily while cradling Zara's head. He stared at her closed eyes and wondered why she was in this place and who the men were. Nothing, save getting her help, mattered; he would think about those issues later.

Carlos said, "Man, she needs a hospital fast. Let's get her out," he said, pulling a knife out of his boot. "Hold her still, Buzz, while I cut the ropes."

After the restraints were sliced away, Carlos scooped up the unconscious woman. "Buzz," he insisted, "lead the way. Jacob, call 911."

Reaching the street, Buzz rushed to the car and opened the back door. He heard Jacob talking on his phone to the police.

"Carlos, we can get her to the hospital faster than waiting for an ambulance. Maybe Jacob can remain here to talk to the detectives."

"Agreed, get in." Carlos carefully draped the battered woman with her head in Buzz's lap. "You keep her steady during the ride while I drive. I'll tell Jacob our plan, and he can meet us there," he added before closing the door.

0 1 0 1 0 1 0 1 0 1 0 1 0 1 0

Buzz paced the worn blue carpet in the remarkably plain hospital waiting room with uncomfortable chairs and tables containing dog-eared magazines from the last decade. He paused when he spotted his oldest friend, Jacob, flanked by a uniformed officer and likely a detective, approaching. He checked his phone, realizing more than an hour had passed.

Carlos stood then finger-combed his black hair before he reached to shake hands with the detective after Buzz introduced himself.

Buzz considered how different yet similar the three of them were. They each topped out at an inch over six feet, in their mid-thirties, with lean, muscular builds. Buzz, the only son of a prominent banker in New York City, hated banking and had studied technology at one of the finest schools. He met Jacob at the university, where they became friends. Jacob earned a full-ride scholarship, while Buzz's family paid in full for his degree. His trust fund kicked in when he graduated, which he took advantage of when he wasn't working. Born and raised in Mexico, Carlos was a communications specialist working with Jacob. These two men came without asking questions when he asked for help to find Zara. He felt they were his only friends,

Buzz and Zara collided on the streets of Manhattan several months ago. The circumstances resulted in him giving her the extra room in his apartment until she could get a job. He'd been living alone for over a year after his girlfriend was murdered. Something stirred in him when he met Zara. During the last six months, he'd grown fond of Zara, realizing this evening exactly how important she was to him.

The police interviewed the trio for an hour. The detective left, promising to interview Zara when she recovered and saying he would call if he needed anything else from them.

"I hope that detective can figure out what happened," Buzz said as he slumped in the hard chair, releasing an exasperated sigh. "I don't understand why she was there or why they hurt her." He rubbed his face and yawned. "She was caught up with the wrong people." He looked around, hoping for a doctor or nurse to appear magically. "I want to know if she's okay. That's all that matters right now."

Jacob, on his left, cleared his throat. "Buzz, I think it's time Carlos and I share a few things with you. Zara's an unusual person with a sketchy background."

Buzz wrinkled his nose with a frown. "What do you mean?"

"You know I work to track hackers and plug security leaks for various customers, including your dad's bank," Jacob said.

Buzz warily nodded, focused intently on his friend, and moving the fingers of his hands, suggested he get to the point.

"I've crossed paths with Zara and her team during several scams I helped uncover."

"No way," Buzz said with a touch of anger. "She wouldn't do that unless she was threatened."

Jacob rested his elbows on his knees and turned his palms up. "Look, I know you don't want to hear this, but she's in it to make a buck, pure and simple."

Buzz groaned. "No, there must be another explanation. She is too sweet to be a bad guy. You're mistaken."

Carlos placed his hand on Buzz's right bicep. "She's a brilliant programmer and sees the big picture, but works as a program contractor for some major players. I discovered her duplicity after she hired me to help supplement a gap in a communications requirement for a contract she promised to deliver. It was a deal for money laundering, which I asked Jacob to look into. She's beautiful, smart, and resourceful, like a fox who wants all the chickens in the henhouse."

Jacob added, "Because of her ability to change her appearance and multiple false identities, she's not on any wanted lists, and I've looked."

Buzz jumped up and stared at the men he trusted like family, frustrated at his poor judgment of people. He realized that what they said didn't matter. She was more important to him than anyone else on the planet. "What are you guys, jealous that I finally have a beautiful woman in my life? I need her. Period."

He wrung his hands and moved a bit as he looked for them to smile or something to take back their lies. The pity he found in their eyes took the fight out of him more than any gut punch he had ever received. He was weary and needed to think. "Guys, thanks for helping me find Zara. I'll stay, but you can both leave now."

Jacob said, "Hey."

Buzz held up his hand for silence. "I need to be alone now. I'll call."

Both stood and shook their heads as they turned and retreated toward the exit. He folded his arms until they were out of sight. Then he sank into the chair to wait for news on her status.

"Mr. Buswald," a nurse called from an open doorway.

He stood. "Yes, ma'am."

"You signed in as next of kin for Zara Zorikoff; how are you related?"

"She's my fiancée and has no living relatives. I verified that we live in Manhattan when I completed the paperwork. What's her status?"

She flipped through the papers in the chart as if looking to verify his statement. "We've moved her to a private room. If you'll follow me, I'll show you the way."

"Thank you. Yes, please. Can you give me details of her condition?"

He bit his lip, realizing she had no intention of answering his question. They entered the elevator and exited on the fourth floor. He followed her brisk pace as she led him through a maze of white walls and vinyl floors, dodging equipment strategically stationed between rooms. He noticed the quiet activity of the staff as he passed the high counters of the nurses' station. His guide pushed open the door to the designated room.

Buzz spotted the figure in the bed and rushed to her side. He stoically stood guard next to her bed, brushing smooth fingertips across her face. Her long eyelashes graced the top of her cheeks, reminding him of her pretty eyes. He was grateful to see the gentle rise and fall of her chest.

An hour later, a doctor entered. "Good evening, Sir. The nurse informed me you're my patient's designated next of kin."

Buzz nodded, "Yes. She's my fiancée, and we live together in Manhattan."

The doctor moved to check her vitals, raised her eyelids to shine light over each eye, and then looked at Buzz. "Ms. Zorikoff had surgery to set the compound fracture of her left arm; she sustained a concussion. We taped her ribs and stitched a couple of her wounds. I expect her to awaken sometime over the next few hours. I'd like her to remain the following day for observation. The nurses will take her stats several times throughout the night. If you stay out of their way, you can remain in the room."

"Thank you. Will she recover?"

"Hard to say at this point, but we'll watch her. She's young. I'll ask the nurse to bring you a pillow and blanket. The chair will lean back if you get tired."

"Thank you, Doc." Throughout the night and into the morning, the continual rhythmic murmurs of her monitoring machines kept Buzz company. He recalled their conversations during their months together. Though Zara hadn't discussed her life, he guessed she was a master of lies and half-truths after what the guys said. Still, he loved her. He wasn't certain why but believed he was irrevocably hooked. Smoothing her hair, he whispered, "I love you, Zara. We'll figure all this out."

After the last nurse's visit, he noticed her eyelids moving but remaining closed. He rested his six-foot wiry frame into the chair not three feet from her side.

0 1 0 1 0 1 0 1 0 1 0 1 0

Zara stirred and released a soft sigh. Throbbing tingles caused discomfort in her extremities, though it seemed to move from one area to another from simply breathing. She heard odd beeps and clicks, then smelled sanitized scents. She sensed crisp sheets that held her in place.

Memories of recent events raced through her mind. She felt the weight of lost opportunities press upon her awakening body. "I prefer the nothingness over the mess I made," she thought. Like a shroud, sadness swept over her body. She felt tears running from the corners of her closed eyes. This beating was worse than when she, as a teen, disobeyed the house mother. But not as bad as the one her widowed father had delivered before selling her to that house. Survival, then and now, remained her prime motivation. "I need to wake up, take control," she internalized. "I must be in a hospital. I need to get alert."

Zara's waking mind replayed the various images of painful acts she first received and then later delivered with the early indoctrination to money and sex. Through these lessons, she learned power and control. An attractive body, honed to a fine instrument of seduction, opened doors for Zara. Some good, others bad, but still, her fortunes changed under the control of a generous benefactor. He enjoyed her body but was intrigued by her brilliant mind. The educational courses and tutors he funded, until she mastered programming technology, made all the difference. She had earned her way out of a life she never requested. Following her patron's death, she found ways to apply her technology knowledge to gain rewards. Big money remained elusive, however, until she took the diamonds. The beating that put her in this hospital crystalized the lesson that stealing only worked if you got away with the prize.

Creaks of weight shifted, possibly from a chair, plus sounds of slow, heavy steps warned her of someone in the room. Despite the pain, she stilled until some knuckles gently stroked her face.

"Zara, you're making noises. Are you awake? It's Buzz. I'd like to see your lovely eyes."

Relief swept through her when she heard no other voices but his. Buzz had given her a place to stay with no strings. She had never had that sort of relationship with anyone. It scared her because she felt sure it would vanish like a dream in the light of day. "How long have I been asleep?"

"Nearly two days since we found you in that apartment in the Bronx. You had surgery to set your arm, stitches, and your ribs are taped. Why did those men beat you, and who are they?"

Zara cringed inside, fearing his shock with an honest response. She ignored his ask. She opened her eyes and then quickly shut away the bright lights. "Thank you for being here." Her words were raspy from her dried throat.

"I wouldn't leave you. The nurse or doctor will likely be in shortly. Do you want a sip of water?"

"Yes." Her eyes opened as slits to get accustomed to the light. "Can you turn off the light?"

He complied.

He held a glass close, and she sipped through the straw, the moisture helping the dryness. Blinking a few more times, her eyes fully opened. At first, relief swept through her that the police were not there, but then a sense of panic set in. "You need to help me leave." She inhaled. "Please."

Buzz pressed the call button attached to her bedside. "Honey, the police will get a call from the doctor now that you are awake. They'll want a statement from you. I told them you called saying you were kidnapped. Do you recall our conversation?"

She closed her eyes, thinking. Moments later, she opened them again and said, "Yes. I gave you a clue, and you must have tracked it to my location. I didn't know if the signal stayed open. Thank you for finding me."

"I am glad we did. There were two men knocked out on the floor. Were they the ones who hurt you? What did they want? How did you know them? I'd like to understand."

"My head hurts. I care about you, but I can't talk about it, maybe ever. I'm sorry." She closed her eyes to block him from seeing her lies.

He patted her arm, and she felt his support, knowing it was not in his nature to pressure her.

A nurse bustled in a few minutes later.

Zara pleaded. "You need to discharge me?"

The nurse chuckled. "You're doing well. I can alert the doctor that all your vitals are in the good range. If he agrees, he'll need to release you." She finished notating the chart and glanced at Zara. "Per the note in your chart, we called the detective in charge of your case. He's on the way for your statement."

Zara nodded, sensing she was trapped.

The doctor entered a scant fifteen minutes later with a chart in hand. He checked her reflexes and her sensitivity to light. "Miss, I think you're a lucky girl after the beating from the mugger. You'll be sore for several weeks because of the deep tissue damage. Don't overdue. Get lots of rest and eat balanced meals. I recommend only gentle exercise for the next three weeks. You should follow up with your physician or return to an emergency room if you have blackouts."

"Thank you."

"You're welcome. Once the police are finished, I'll complete the discharge papers. The nurse will bring them to you. Take care. This young man, I feel certain, will take care of you. He's barely left your side."

The conversation with the detective was easier than she had expected. She identified her attackers from photos the detective showed her. Then, she fabricated a believable tale from what Buzz told her about his interrogation by the detective, along with that of his friends. Buzz quietly sat beside her, holding her hand, rubbing his thumb over the top of her hand.

"You may be called to testify. We had enough to jail the two. They'll be on ice for a while."

"Thank you," she said with a slight rise to her lips. "May I go home now?"

"Yes, ma'am. We're finished. I hope you recover from your ordeal."

0101010101010

Buzz escorted her back to his New York apartment, ensuring she was comfortable. At the door, he scraped his black curly hair back with one hand and pulled his key from his dress jeans before he said, "I'd like you to stay here. You mean a great deal to me. I can't lose you. I won't ask questions until you're ready to talk. I'll watch over you. Everyone makes mistakes. Lord knows I've had my share."

With only slight encouragement, Zara spent most of her time resting for the next several weeks. She started to regain strength, spending more time awake. He took care of the chores and delivered meals to her in bed. One night, she ventured into the kitchen dressed.

"Zara," he grinned, sensing his love for her bouncing up a notch and pleased with her surprise, "you look much better. Have a seat at the bar while I cook. You've finished all your medications. Would you like a glass of wine?"

"Sounds good." She flashed a smile. "What are you fixing?"

He passed her a glass and raised his. "To us, pretty lady, and our future if you want it."

The tone of the glasses made him grin. He took a sip, set the glass to the side, and waved his hands with a flourish over the fresh vegetables he had recently rinsed. "I thought stir fry would be a nice change and provide some good leftovers." He grabbed the cutting board and his favorite knife, working through the colorful variety with even cuts.

"The fresh food smells fantastic even before it's cooked," she said with a smile. "You never cease to amaze me with your hidden talents."

The oil sizzling welcomed the sliced veggies, releasing a different fragrance. He chuckled when the growl from her stomach announced her hunger. "I'm delighted you have an appetite. Would you prefer shrimp or chicken?"

"Either is fine with me. It smells incredible."

They enjoyed the meal and then retired.

0 1 0 1 0 1 0 1 0 1 0 1 0 1 0

Their relationship began to resemble what they had before the incident. He did a bit of remote programming but spent most of the day caring for her needs. He hired a physical therapist who stopped in a couple of times per week. He aimed to put all the demons behind them and move on with a life together. They shared the same bed but weren't the same couple. He was more in love than ever for reasons he couldn't explain.

Buzz woke first each morning. He liked to see her thick ebony hair that flowed into a mass of waves spilling onto the pillow and cradling the flawless, creamy skin of her lovely face. The physical bruises faded, yet Buzz felt she ignored her emotional damage. He almost hoped she'd talk in her sleep and explain her mental demons.

Zara opened her eyes. Spotting him, she whispered, "Good morning, Buzz, how did I rest?"

Buzz grinned. "You rested well and only kicked me once during the night. What would you like to do today? Walk in the park, program up a storm, marry me and run away to a tropical island, or tell me some things I don't know about you."

Zara lowered her eyelids and tapped his chin to mull over her options. Looking up, it seemed as if he was searching his soul. She looked deep into his dark eyes. "I think it's time I told you a portion of my past. Then I'd like to hear more about your tropical island idea."

"All right." He noticed her Russian accent was a bit more pronounced. He settled against the headboard and pulled up the sheets.

Zara cleared her throat. "I don't want to go too far back in my history. It's not something I like to think about. I've done many things I'm not proud of, but survived. I didn't know nice people were real. I've lied, cheated, and compromised myself for far too long. I wanted to get the big payoff from the diamonds I'd stolen from the thief, then escape." She reached over for his hand. "Then, you came into my life or tripped over me." She chuckled. "Funny how little the gems mattered after I met you. You, Buzz, are the wild card without boundaries for me."

"Will you tell me how the men who beat you were neutralized?" Buzz pressed.

Gently but firmly, she replied, "I don't know. They took me to learn the diamonds' whereabouts and punish me. They have the diamonds and no reason to think I'm even alive. Thankfully, that life is gone for me. The rest is irrelevant." She stretched and settled against his shoulder. "If you want us to be together, we must look forward. I love you and want to stay with you. I suspect you have feelings for me, especially because you tell me daily. I don't want to get married, but I'm pleased you asked."

Surprised by her candor, Buzz grinned. "None of us is perfect. I couldn't follow in my father's footsteps, even after years of education and unlimited chances to succeed. I loved someone who got killed by some maniac. I'm not particularly eager to look too closely at my past either. Frankly, I only want you." He kissed her cheek. "I'm an average programmer. I've often taken the easy path and paid the price. We're quite a pair, aren't we?"

Zara nodded in agreement, wrapping her arms around him. She hugged him closer than she had in weeks. "I'll stick to the truth going forward, but I can't share all my past."

"Then, my Zara, we begin from this minute. Now, about the trip?"

Buzz insisted that Zara help make arrangements to begin their travels. They boarded a flight to San Juan, Puerto Rico, First Class. Once in the air, the flight attendant took their drink requests. When the drinks arrived, Buzz toasted. "Sweetheart, this is our new life. I was so lucky you ran into me that day on the sidewalk. You arrived at a time when I was unsure of my next step. Getting this far hasn't been easy for us." He raised his glass. "Here's to us!"

Their glasses touched with affectionate smiles exchanged.

"I hope one day you'll reconsider marrying me. I see a great life in our future. We might start a family."

"Buzz, darling, I'm glad we're making a fresh start somewhere new. I don't want to worry about my…our past." She stared at him. "Marriage may be in our future. But, I'm uncertain about having children."

"All I want is you. I need you in my life. I won't force anything on you. At some point in my life, I want to look down at my child and see your features."

Zara leaned over and kissed him, sending passion straight to his heart and relieving some of his anxiety. He was hopeful they had turned a corner together.

0 1 0 1 0 1 0 1 0 1 0 1 0 1 0

A few days after arriving in San Juan, they located a small house at the city's edge and settled in. They made several sojourns to neighboring islands, exploring many local features. Zara was surprised at how much she liked each island's historical aspects, meeting new people and hearing their stories. It was a different lifestyle than either of them had experienced. They grew closer each day. Buzz realized he could take on adult responsibilities while living off his trust fund.

Buzz enjoyed their forays to different parts of the city. They met many locals. He enjoyed watching Zara engage with the women and inquire about their children. She remembered the names of everyone they met, citing their family history chapter and verse.

One fascinating person who crossed their path was a professor from the university, Sebastian. They met him one evening at a popular spot within walking distance of their bungalow. It was a Friday, and the twenty tables inside and out were filled. The interior had bright colors typical of the area. The food was delicious, the drinks were well made, and the music was a live vocalist they had not heard sing before. Buzz noticed the portly man in a rumpled suit about his father's age carrying a glass of red wine, searching for something.

Buzz asked as the man paused nearby, "Sir, are you meeting friends or searching for a spot to sit?"

The man broadly smiled. "I need a seat to order food. I'm starved."

Buzz gestured easily. "Come sit with us. Tell us about yourself." Buzz liked the appreciative glance the man gave Zara as he extended his hand in greeting.

"You are lovely, ma'am. I notice your glass is empty. If you and your dinner partner will allow me to join, I'd be honored to fill your glass and swap stories."

Zara laughed and said, "Honey, you were right. He needs to join us."

Buzz extended his hand. "My name is Buzz. This lovely lady is Zara. We moved to your fair city to explore it and the surrounding islands. I am a part-time programmer."

The man sat and signaled the waiter for a round of drinks. "My name is Professor Morales, but call me Sebastian. Technically, I'm the dean of the Instituto Tecnologico de Puerto Rico-Recinto de San Juan, the local university. I am single, enjoy soccer, and know most of the students. I enjoy teaching and often learn something new each semester."

Buzz watched Zara's eyes light up as the subject sparked her interest.

"What courses do you prefer, Professor?" she asked.

"Call me Sebastian, please, Zara. I think we'll be best of friends. I teach technology courses as I have a passion for the field. We must ensure our children understand how to get along in our modern age."

"We agree," Buzz said. "We both have technology backgrounds."

Zara grinned. "I'm not working at present like Buzz is. I am learning a lot about the history of this region in the Caribbean. I love it here."

The three of them closed the bar and exchanged numbers. It became the first of many meals they would share. It became a weekly event to meet up to share a meal and swap stories if they weren't traveling to an adjacent island.

Buzz also enjoyed spoiling Zara. He still cooked many of their meals but enjoyed planning dinner and drinks in romantic settings. He would invariably press his case during dessert, hoping for a sweet response.

He would look into her eyes when he asked, "Darling, are you ready to make an honest man of me? We could have a ceremony here with the local priest. You'd look so lovely with flowers woven in your long hair."

She playfully swatted his arm and laughed. "We'll talk about it another time, honey. You're happy now, right?"

"Yes. I'm happy with you, but…"

And she'd lean over and kiss the thoughts away, then hold his hand. His heart soared with happiness, but he still wanted more.

0 1 0 1 0 1 0 1 0 1 0 1 0 1 0

They enjoyed short forays to other islands for over a year, using San Juan as their base. When they returned from their latest weekend getaway that afternoon, Buzz made Bistec Encebollado while Zara unpacked and started laundry. He marinated the steak while slicing the onions. The dish was simple but bursting with spicy flavor. It worked well with rice on the side.

Buzz figured Zara must have finished the unpacking when she sashayed into the kitchen, kissing him quickly.

"How about a red wine with that wonderful meal you're fixing? Then I'll set the table."

He grinned at the ease of their division of chores. "I like how you think, my dear. Red works. We have so much fun together, whether traveling to see surrounding places or eating dinner." Buzz braised the meat and added the fresh onions. The Caribbean spices they were both fond of filled the air.

"I agree. How long can we stay here? We've never discussed a time limit. I think it's time I find a job." Zara set the table with bright placemats, plates, and napkins. She grabbed the flowers purchased on the way home from the pier and added water to a complimentary vase, setting it in the corner.

"With the monthly allocation from my investments and the trust fund, we're good for as long as you wish. We work together so well, and we have fun. We've put the past behind us and created a delightful life. Being with you is fun. Are you bored?"

"No, I'm having fun. But I would like to contribute. I get excited when Sebastian talks about his classes and students. I wonder if we are missing something."

"An interesting thought." He chuckled. "This meal is about ready; hope you're hungry. Tell me what you're thinking of while we eat."

They sat and savored each bite while recanting the adventures shared during the recent trip.

"This is yummy," she said with a grin. "I find it amazing how basic ingredients make the best meals. Buzz, I wonder how we might give back to this place that makes us feel so good."

He nodded, "We've become so close."

"We have." Her brow furrowed. "San Juan and other island tourist cities are best known for the bars, casinos, and nightclubs. We've become acquainted with many of the locals."

"True. Parents here want their children to get educated, even college or technical training." He stabbed the steak and chewed another bite, savoring the tender flavor.

"Exactly; Miquel Torres said his son is planning to teach, and Sondra Diaz has a daughter who wants to attend university, but it's so expensive."

"Now that we have no other travel planned for a while let's have supper with Sebastian. Perhaps we could teach there and sponsor one or two young people annually. We're technologists. You have a great understanding of the latest and greatest. Sebastian loves conversing with us. You are diligent in knowing the technology shifts better than me."

Zara took the last forkful and chewed. "I think you're right. We could teach. We could help youngsters learn from the ground up with experiential training." She rubbed her hands together, and he noticed her animation. "Please call him Buzz. We might be able to convince him."

Buzz went to grab his cell phone. When he returned, he discovered Zara had cleared the table and poured an extra glass of wine for both. He thumbed through his contacts until he located his target. The call connected. "Sebastian, it's Buzz, how are you? Zara and I wondered if you'd join us for dinner tomorrow?" He nodded toward Zara as he listened. "Oh, that sounds interesting. Sure, we'll see you there tomorrow at six. Thanks."

"That sounded a bit odd. What did he say."

"He was delighted I called because he wanted to speak to us regarding his new idea."

She smiled. "Maybe we have good timing."

He reached over and pulled her hand into his. "That would be a good thing."

0101010101010

The weather was warm, with a gentle breeze, so they strolled. Buzz, dressed in tan shorts and a short-sleeved purple shirt, held hands with Zara. Her flowered-print summer dress graced her long legs. They arrived at Jungle Bird a few minutes before six. They selected a table outside and looked at the menu.

Sebastian arrived with all smiles right on time. His white linen slacks were topped with a tropical print shirt, a bit tight due to his girth. Buzz knew if the professor laughed, he might risk losing a button like he had the last time they shared a meal. They both stood as he approached the table.

"There you are, my favorite people. So glad you're back." He gave Zara a friendly hug and back-slapped Buzz. "How was your recent trip? Did you have fun snorkeling and lounging on the beach? It wasn't the same without you here."

"It was a good trip," Zara said with a smile. "I can grab our drinks if you tell me what you want."

"Oh, goodness, yes," Sebastian said.

"Me too," added Buzz. "Thank you, honey."

"When Zara comes back, I want your thoughts on my idea. You are both so good in tech that I'd like to hire you."

Buzz noticed the man's dark eyes twinkling as his smile broadened. "Zara and I discussed last night that we want to give back to the city which has helped us."

"Good," Sebastian laughed aloud before noticing Zara returning. "Thank you for getting our drinks. Let's have a toast to discuss the art of the possible." He grinned and raised a glass.

"Cheers." They said in unison.

"I can't wait to hear your idea, Sebastian," Buzz said.

"All our discussions made me think about how education could shift to match technology changes. I don't mean robotics, but that might be in the future. We could train them on practical skills that would help them become ready to step into jobs even here in San Juan. If we offer more here, we can keep our young people and grow. You mentioned working in New York and even internationally when we first met. San Juan would be newer in technology innovation field, but I think it is a good time for our youth to get on board."

Buzz noticed, as usual, that the professor's hands added to the conversation as he became more excited and the speed of his speech increased.

"I recently received some grants for the university to expand the course curriculum with a focus on innovation. I want to offer hands-on labs as part of the studies for two study tracks, Information Technology and Systems Security." He took a sip of his Old Cuban and added an extra breath.

Zara looked like she would burst if she couldn't talk, so Buzz nodded for her to start.

"Professor, we talked about wanting to find you and perhaps help teach. Your idea is perfect for us to help the young people on the island."

"It's so neat that you got a grant. We'd love to help you," interjected Buzz.

"I have two locations already under consideration. I'd like you to help review them for suitability for practical labs. I'd like you two to head up the off-campus labs here in San Juan at a modest salary. It might reduce travel time, but the university breaks would be yours."

"Sebastian, this sounds exciting and aligned with what we discussed. Do you think the students could build the lab network infrastructure?" Zara asked.

"Ideally, I want to expose students to all aspects of technology, guided by Madam Zara and el Señor Buzz." His hands encompassed them. He hooted uproariously. "Tell me you'll consider the idea."

Buzz wrapped his hand over Zara's and grinned. "We'll accept your generous offer. How would these off-site locations interact with the university?"

"I envision these technology hubs networked to optimize the university's resources. To ensure spending integrity, I will provide funds oversight, but your ideas and plans will get my highest consideration."

Zara eagerly agreed with this approach. "You're right, Professor," she said. "This is the best way to understand technology thoroughly. It is how I learned. We can teach it all with our experience in programming and data centers. Buzz also has connections for placing graduated students in reasonable jobs stateside. We'll create an excellent learning experience."

Buzz loved her pronounced excitement about the project.

Sebastian finished his drink and stood. "I would love to stay, but I have papers to grade. I look forward to your answer when we meet at noon tomorrow."

They shook hands. Buzz watched the man until he disappeared. Zara and Buzz stayed at the restaurant until it closed. They were too wired to sleep, so they continued the discussion after getting home.

"I must admit that being out of work has made me restless," Zara confessed. "I've enjoyed our wanderings together around the islands. But I need purpose. This job offer from Sebastian is… it is something I… we can do well."

Buzz was enchanted with the spark that lit up her eyes. Before they retired, Buzz mused, "Zara, this is a great plan for our future. Marry me, and let's start a family. Together, we can build this education empire for our children."

Zara sighed. "Buzz, there is so much to get done with locating the labs and planning their layout and connectivity. We won't have time to take care of a baby. Perhaps later." Zara kissed him. They pursued passionate lovemaking until they both drifted into a satisfied slumber.

0 1 0 1 0 1 0 1 0 1 0 1 0 1 0

She woke first and watched him in the early morning light. As he stirred, Zara leaned over and kissed his cheek. He pulled her into a warm embrace.

"Darling," Zara purred, her Russian accent rolling off her tongue. "How do you always know when I wish you to hold me?"

Buzz chuckled. "Why are you always so desirable when you first wake?"

She hugged him back as she snuggled closer for another session of lovemaking. Following this delightful romp, they shared a shower. Then they dressed and walked hand in hand toward the local café for breakfast. Buzz loved having this beautiful lady beside him. Zara was dressed in a brown printed summer dress tied behind her neck and cinched at the waist. The flared hemline brushed her legs just above her knees as she walked. Buzz sauntered along in navy shorts and a light blue striped short-sleeved shirt. Both wore sandals that had walked many miles.

An outside table was available. They sat down. A waiter arrived with two coffees and menus.

"Good morning, folks. Lovely day. What do you feel like this morning?"

Zara took a savory sip of coffee and grinned at the waiter. "Any recommendations, Rico? You always make the best recommendations."

"I agree. Rico, surprise us with your best suggestion for me and my girl."

The waiter bowed and retrieved the menus as he went inside. They often came here for breakfast because the food and the walk were pleasant. It was early, and no tourists were about to disturb the peaceful morning.

"My darling Buzz, how did you sleep? Did you dream about our new opportunity? I don't know about you, but I'm ready to work on this project."

"I slept well. I dreamt about a room full of students like in college and cringed at the students' antics. With your experience leading a team, this is a perfect prospect. I'm afraid I may have exaggerated my skills slightly."

Zara leaned toward him and patted his arm. "Darling, we're adults. We all exaggerate to one degree or another. You have many skills. Together, we will teach these young people real skills. When they graduate, they will have a better chance…"

Falling silent, she stared off, thinking of the past where violence and manipulation had ruled. She kicked herself to remember her accomplishments. She had proven she had a talent for technical programming and project management. She liked young people and often worked to help them. She hesitated to tell him how much his support today meant. A shadow of worry crossed his face, but he smiled as she returned his glance.

"Wow, you drifted somewhere else for a moment. Is there anything you want to share? You can tell me anything, you know."

Removing her hand, Zara shook her head and smiled. "All is good, here with you. Sometimes, my mind plays tricks with my memories. I don't want to dredge up ancient history. With you, I'm safe."

"All right. I agree. It is a past from before we met, and I promised to move forward." He squeezed her hand. "What time are we to meet up with Sebastian?"

"We're to meet him before noon. He'll text us the address."

"Do you think this will be our future, Buzz? This whole idea is wonderful, even if a bit too good to be real. We won't be rich, but can give back like we discussed. I'm uncertain if I will influence young adults best."

"I don't know about the future, Zara. I am glad we can try. You'll be wonderful with your drive for perfection."

Zara frowned and thought for a moment. "Programs are logical and should be flawless. I also know that the more one writes, the better one gets. We must plan to make these students the best they can be."

Breakfast arrived, and the surprise was amazing. Rico had outdone himself yet again with Papas con Huevos. He warmed their coffee and beamed at their compliments. They laughed at jokes between bites of the tasty potatoes and eggs. They watched as the shops opened and street musicians gathered. The first tourist ship was due to arrive at the harbor soon. Certain city areas were common targets of tourists, and residents knew how to avoid the crush. When the text arrived from Sebastian, they finished their coffee and settled up. Walking to the designated location would take less than thirty minutes.

Sebastian was visible through the open door of the nondescript building. None of the color or grill work prevalent in San Juan graced the structure. Zara quickened her pace and broke free of Buzz's hand to rush inside. There were a few small windows within inches of the twelve-foot ceiling.

Zara pointed out that the beige walls had no graffiti, indicating the gangs hadn't discovered it was empty. The door opened to a large space surrounded by six smaller rooms. Each of the smaller rooms had doors that allowed access and privacy.

"Sebastian!" Zara declared. "These rooms will be perfect for meetings, consultations, and study pairs. Adding whiteboards in each of the small rooms would be useful."

Sebastian was busy scribbling notes. Buzz went to the big room to check the flooring and the electrical closet nestled into the corner.

He returned a few minutes later. "I stepped off the size of the room. It would be safer to build a raised floor to nestle the cables. There appears to be enough electricity. We need to verify the cooling requirements based on the quantity of servers planned. Can the school's electrician do this, Sebastian?"

Zara nodded. "That makes perfect sense to me."

Sebastian grinned and admired their detailed observations.

"Would you two like a small refrigerator and microwave in the kitchenette, too? There is a cupboard for cups and such."

Zara beamed, dancing with excitement. "This is perfect, Sebastian. Can we get started with plans tonight? Buzz and I can draw up what we would like and a list of equipment. When can we get the students? There is a lot to do, but the sooner we start, the faster we can make your dream a reality."

Zara noticed Buzz looking from the room to the ceiling and cocking his head in thought.

He stated, "The raised floor will be great for cooling and cabling. Yet, if we bolt the frames to the floor and run all the cables overhead, all we'd need is a ladder. It would make it easy to dismantle and reconfigure for each class. We can cover data center and cloud theory in the lectures and keep our installation modest."

"Buzz is right, Sebastian. It would make it easy to train and evolve with changes in the field."

Sebastian rubbed his chin, contemplating for several moments before replying. "It might be good for the first class in each lab to have that experience." For the next few minutes, he provided extra details about what could and could not happen with the funding.

Zara nodded, then looked to Buzz. "I agree with Sebastian, Buzz. This can be a well-utilized space with planning."

"Sebastian, how does the other property compare? And did you find a third one, or are we starting with two?" Buzz asked.

"You two are not Caribbean natives." He laughed good-naturedly. "You don't waste any time. The other building is nearly the same but has one extra-long room and an outside patio area. I stopped there on the way over as it was closer to my home. Do you want to see it or complete the plans for this one first? If I lease it, I get a better rate for fifteen years. How many years would you be willing to commit to?"

Zara looked at Buzz. "I don't know, Sebastian. What would you prefer?"

"How about we start with a two-year commitment followed by five-year options? We can learn how we work together."

"I don't know."

Buzz interjected, "I like his idea, Zara. It makes sense to start slow and then grow. If Sebastian decides on other possibilities for this space, we can agree yet remain friends. It makes sense that we consider and nominate graduated students from each location to manage the operation of their lab as a capstone class. We can oversee. The experience will be invaluable to their careers. That makes it easier to provide references when placing them into jobs."

Sebastian immediately brightened and gave them each a hearty handshake. "That's a deal. This is our contract, and I will write up the paperwork with the details tonight. As soon as you both sign, everything will move forward for approval by the President of the College Board. He has decided this is his pet project," Sebastian grinned.

"Let's go inspect the other property, and then we both have our assignments for this evening. Welcome aboard, professors. This is going to be exciting."

Buzz grinned at Zara and recounted, "I like us as Professors."

They walked over to the next building. Buzz and Zara were delighted; Sebastian's description was spot on. Between all the talking, the ideas were flowing, each one better than the one before. They promised to meet the following afternoon. Sebastian left in a hurry to meet with the real estate agent to discuss the terms of the leases to give to the President of the College Board.

Zara talked all the way home, dancing around and prioritizing her to-do list. She stopped to hug Buzz more than once during their walk home. Her world seemed on the right trajectory for once.

"Darling, let's stop and pick up some food and extra wine on the way home. We can eat and write our plan."

"Yes, darling," she said with a grin. "Ideas are filling my head. I was hoping we could stay in." She rushed inside to start drafting the plans.

He started their dinner.

0 1 0 1 0 1 0 1 0 1 0 1 0 1 0

Buzz set the table and brought out the serving dishes. He noticed she was focused on the project using their coffee table. He walked over to her work area. "Sweetheart, your detailed plans for the wiring, room modifications, network configuration, and the high-level curriculum will wow Sebastian. I'm glad we have this opportunity to share. You seem so pleased." He handed her a glass of wine and winked. "How about we tie the knot over the weekend."

Zara laughed and stood. "Sweetheart, we'll get married some-time. Let's eat. I can smell your delicious concoction, and my stomach is growling."

They sat, and she raised her glass. "Buzz, you said you love me the way I am. We need to stay focused to avoid messing up this unbelievable opportunity." Zara looked seductively at Buzz as she licked her lips. "Save a bit of passion for later, honey. You made all this possible. Thank you." She clicked his glass.

When they finished their meal, she leaned over and kissed his cheek. Then she rose and returned to the drawings and notes. He heard her furious scribbles as he cleared the dishes, happy to see her so engaged. He wished he could figure out a way to get her to marry him.

The next day, they met with Sebastian, reviewed the fine print, and signed the employment contracts. Zara rolled out the plans and provided a detailed list of the needed materials for the lab.

"These are fantastic. I will get the orders for the material under-way this afternoon. I thought about your five-year options and decided that if worse came to worse, I could offer the top students to take over if you leave. Your detail convinces me that you two will bring my vision of innovative technology education at the university to life."

Buzz replied, "Zara is the mastermind behind this design. We are both committed to working with you and helping your students."

"We're so excited," Zara said.

"Walk with me to the city offices to pick up the leases. I have a meeting with the president later today to explain how twenty years gave us the best price."

"The monthly lease amount looks amazing; your grantees will be pleased," added Buzz.

"I agree. After I sign the commitment, let's celebrate with a dinner at any local place you choose, Madam Zara. My treat."

0 1 0 1 0 1 0 1 0 1 0 1 0 1 0

The first semester went off without a hitch, with ten young men accepted in class. The course required attendance was three days per week, seven hours per day, with a combination of lab and lecture work. Zara and Buzz both pitched in to run the overhead cables. During the first week, one young man was overheard commenting to his classmates. "Madam Zara could do far more than teach a geek class, if you know what I mean." The group all snickered.

Buzz was ready to step in to defend her honor.

Bemused, Zara sashayed up to the group. "Young man," her head tilted, leveling her gaze at the mouthy jerk. "Don't be insulting. You're a little boy with potential based on your grades. I promise you'll meet women who will join your ranks and have greater expertise than you. You'll have a chance to learn together in a field that changes exponentially daily. Don't start your career with disparaging or suggestive sexual comments that might cost you a nice technical profession. The business world won't tolerate it, and neither will this university."

Buzz grinned at the startled look on the young man, Mark. He mumbled an apology, looking at the floor, likely hoping it would open up and swallow him.

Mark headed up the team that won the capstone final many months later. He accepted the trophy. "I want to express gratitude on behalf of the team to Madam Zara and el Señor Buzz for making us work hard. I learned more than I expected, and the team did, too. I look forward to recommending this course to others.

"Madam Zara, thank you for straightening me out early on. Young women will make a positive impact in this industry. It's been an honor to learn from you."

Sebastian took the class to dinner to mark the achievements of the graduates of the first of these classes. He praised their efforts and toasted their continued success.

"I'm delighted with the innovations you both made," Sebastian proclaimed after the students left. "Eight students secured top jobs with Buzz's letters of recommendation. The other two students indicated they were partnering in a start-up consulting company."

Later that night at home, Zara commented. "I never expected Mark to act so grown up in such a short time. I find that remarkable."

Buzz reached his arm over her shoulder and pulled her close. He smiled. "Zara, you're an incredible woman and mentor. We have found a great place to call home. Marry me, darling, and we'll build our family here."

Zara suddenly appeared so sad as she shook her head ever so slightly. He was stunned into silence.

"Buzz, why do you try to change all that we are? We're happy and making our way. I don't want anything to change our positive outlook. Honestly, I have never felt this good. Please, don't make me choose."

Buzz was crestfallen but not beaten. "Honey, you can't blame me for trying. I'll want you for my wife as long as I live. You can't push me away forever. Don't be surprised when I ask again. I'm a bit stubborn on some things." He cleared his throat. "To change the subject, I'll second Mark's statements about your teaching. I, too, have learned a great deal from you. I surprised myself at how much I've improved. Next semester, I'll work on some new course materials. I want to lead the network infrastructure build-out in the second location."

Zara appeared relieved to shift topics. More animated, she replied, "I agree. You're programming skills needed refining. We're going to do even more next year and the year after.

"For the networking of the secondary location, I wanted your thoughts on …"

They spent hours outlining the grandiose plans Zara envisioned for the two labs. Buzz wrote up the phases for Sebastian to review and approve. An expansion of the curriculum was also approved, which delighted Zara.

0 1 0 1 0 1 0 1 0 1 0 1 0 1 0

Good news travels fast. The next group of students must have heard the comments from the prior class. The new students were enthusiastic during the introductions. The gender mix shifted, with three of the twelve students being women. The first day the young women sauntered in, Zara read them perfectly. She'd learned her people reading skills during her first years trapped in the Russian brothel.

The feisty, sassy, white-blonde Judith was pretty, with bright eyes, a quick smile, and a carefree style. Xiamara, the confident brunette, walked in with an undefined edge as she checked out every guy in class. Everyone felt she was ranking her prey. This left Zara speculating what the position order was based upon. Lastly, Marci wore her fiery red hair like a mane, which she moved with practiced seduction. These women would be a challenge to the young men, but Zara wasn't certain they would compete fairly. The mix of students meant more knowledge would be gained by splitting up into new teams. This would also force the young men to appreciate the ideas these women could bring to projects.

The teams settled in with Judith and Xiamara in the scoring lead. Their ideas and innovations were unconventional yet sound. The teams learned respect for the various contributions everyone made. The women rebuked all romantic advances by the young men in various ways. Marci struggled near the lower end of the grading. Halfway through the semester, she resigned. Zara felt it personally when the reasons for quitting weren't explained.

At the semester's end, Judith gave the closing speech to the class, and they all hugged one another in turn. Judith and Xiamara invited Zara and Buzz to dinner as a thank-you. Sebastian ended up joining the little party. A couple of toasts later, Judith tapped her glass to gain everyone's attention.

"Madam Zara and el Señor Buzz, you have given us a great foundation for our technology careers. Xiamara and I can get even better working with you for another year. We want to be your techs and teachers' aides."

Sebastian beamed. Buzz grinned. Zara looked at the two women with no expression. "You both did quite well during the training. To be on our staff, we expect a little less cowboy and a little more contribution to the university. Is that something you could commit to doing?"

Both girls grinned and squealed in unison. "Yes, Madam Zara!"

Judith continued, "We'll help with the network, programming, web design, and workshops. The ideas we have will be revolutionary!"

Sebastian interjected, "I appreciate your exuberance. But I need to check the budget before approving your work for the university, even in the labs.

"Zara, Buzz, do you need the help at this point, or do we need to discuss this privately?"

Buzz looked back and forth between the eager faces. "We can use the help. The security connections between these locations and back to the university are critical. From that perspective, we can build a business plan for part-time work for each of them. From time to time, we might need more hours."

Xiamara exclaimed, "We can even create a revenue stream for the university off the website. I discussed some ideas with Judith, who agrees with me."

Zara did a hard stare at both of these talented women. "As long as it is not illegal, immoral, or a security risk, I would consider it a good investment, Sebastian. I'll double-check their work. Ladies, if you can get around our safeguards, think again, and don't waste our time."

They all shook hands in agreement.

After Buzz and Zara showered and snuggled into bed, Buzz asked, "Now that we have this help, will you marry me, Zara? Stay with me forever."

"Isn't our life together good? Let's discuss this later. Right now, make love to me." She deepened his distraction. She remembered learning how to service men to avoid beatings. Zara prayed Buzz was not that sort of man, but she never wanted to risk it with a child of theirs.

Zara was relieved as the productive semesters in Puerto Rico continued. They built a respectable life teaching the local youth as next-generation technologists. Their roles allowed them to maintain their technology edge, one page ahead of the class. Every year following graduation, Buzz repeated his request.

Zara said, "We are happy together, aren't we?"

"Yes, we are. I can't wait for the semester break to take you to St. Kitts and relax on the beach, sample new foods, and," he wiggled his eyebrows with the sweet little boy grin, "wrap you in my arms at night."

She reached in for a hug, adding a passionate kiss. "Then let's be us and stay happy."

0101010101010

At the beginning of the next semester, their world shifted when a hurricane struck Puerto Rico, leaving a swath of devastation in its path. People were left homeless, with survival as the primary concern. Former and current students helped clear the rubble from the buildings in the aftermath. Using a couple of commercial generators, the labs became a hub for communication in and out of San Juan. Though classes were suspended, Sebastian's programs received accolades from the leaders of Puerto Rico. Sebastian publicly credited Madam Zara and el Señor Buzz with their insight into technology inroads. They were pleased.

One of their former students, Mark, asked them both to dinner. After weeks of backbreaking work, going out for dinner was a treat.

Buzz finished his shower and toweled off. He smiled at Zara as she carefully applied a little makeup and brushed out her lovely hair. "You look pretty," he grinned.

"Thank you." Her eyes caught him in the mirror. "I wonder why Mark would invite us to dinner, but I am glad. He's very successful these days and yet spent time helping with our efforts to keep communications open."

Buzz began dressing. "I am curious but not one to turn down a free meal. We'll find out soon. Perhaps we can dance a little tonight and share stories."

She nodded with a sly smile.

A short time later, they arrived at the restaurant. Mark met them at one of the few bars operational since the storm. They shook hands, and he introduced them to the woman beside him. "I'm not certain if you remember Marci. She entered your class but decided not to pursue it."

Buzz felt stunned. The young woman appeared confident and poised, standing beside Mark and holding his hand. He couldn't miss the modest diamond on her finger.

"Marci," Zara said, "you have a happy glow about you. I often wondered what became of you."

Marci reached over and hugged Zara. "Let's find our table, and I'll tell you."

The women sat next to one another. After they placed their order, Marci shared her background. "It's sort of funny. I knew Mark and had a mad crush on him. When he said how wonderful your training was, I thought I could make him notice me if I took the class. You see, he promised to tutor the students on the side if they got confused."

Buzz looked at Mark and play-punched his arm, "You did grow up that year. Well done."

Mark smirked. "I did. Marci came to me for tutoring. She said she didn't enjoy it, and the other girls in class were much better."

Buzz watched Zara arch one eye before she stated, "But you were flirting with him."

Marci nodded with a slight blush rising from her neck. "That was exactly how it started. Mark helped me understand that technology wasn't my thing. He got me a job in the marketing department at his company. On day one, I was enthralled with the power of marketing. We've collaborated ever since. He's starting his own business providing internet services to the region. I'll get to do the marketing."

Mark squeezed her hand. "That's not why we invited you, however. I wanted to thank you both for changing my life. I'm at the pinnacle of my profession because of your teachings. el Señor Buzz, my parents are both gone, and I would like you to stand up as my Best Man at our wedding next Sunday."

Marci raised her hand to each of them. "We're so happy. We plan to start a family soon after the business is established."

"I have a contract with the university, thanks to Sebastian." Mark raised a glass to everyone. "Without you two, I would not have this opportunity. I want Marci and me to be as happy as you."

Buzz and Zara returned home. She chattered about the upcoming wedding and his being asked to help in the ceremony. He was unexpectedly jealous of Mark and needed to try harder to convince Zara they should be married.

0 1 0 1 0 1 0 1 0 1 0 1 0 1 0

Their lives fell into a usual routine of teaching and mentoring students. This was gratifying to both of them. Often as not, Zara would notice Buzz staring off into space with a faraway look steeped in melancholy. She was certain he lamented not having a legitimate family, so she never asked him to explain. Zara knew he would only ask her why not, and then the prying into her past would begin again.

Zara realized the riff between them, born of hidden pasts and hurt feelings, was growing. They spent less time exploring the surrounding locals, and laughter became a thing of the past. She did her best to praise his successes, yet they drifted apart. They were agreeable, but the spark seemed to have winked out. They were cordial but not as spontaneous or loving. When she looked in the mirror and spotted strands of grey, she decided it was age-related. They still worked well together.

They were both pleased with the jobs Buzz's references helped secure for their graduates. Zara rushed home after the paperwork and semester-end teardown of the lab were completed to bathe and prepare for the traditional graduation dinner. Sebastian had pestered them to sign a new five-year agreement.

Buzz texted her, saying he stopped with a few graduates for a quick snack and beverage at the local bar. When he arrived, she greeted him at the door, perfectly outfitted in a short dress with a gathered skirt that swayed as she walked. Buzz's kiss nearly met her lips. She raised an eyebrow after smelling his breath.

"You might want to change before we head for dinner with Sebastian."

"All right." Buzz took a fast shower. He emerged with his hair combed and new clothes suitable for the chosen restaurant.

They walked to the restaurant, each lost in their thoughts.

Zara watched as Buzz, mindful of his drinking limits, alternated between water and wine during dinner.

"Yet again, you both have succeeded in helping our students complete their coursework. I loved the additional cloud technology elements you added to the semester."

Zara clicked Sebastian's glass and said, "Buzz was instrumental in that facet of the labs and secured some awesome new-hire positions for the students. The school's reputation gives students a leg up in the battle for high-paying jobs."

Zara watched Buzz stare off in the distance, surprised when he insisted on dessert.

"It's been a good year," Buzz agreed. "We need to sign the new contract, right?"

"Yes," replied Sebastian. "But first, you two haven't been off the island for some time. Take a long vacation. Go explore some new snorkeling and see if the fishes missed you." He laughed loudly, his generous stomach jiggling.

"What a great idea. We'll return after our honeymoon, ready to get the new group of students ready to compete in the job market."

Sebastian blinked in surprise. "Congratulations. This calls for another drink."

Zara smiled but declined as she rose. "We need to get home and plan our travel. I'm not certain when we are leaving. Thank you for dinner, Sebastian." She hugged the old professor, spotting the grey and white mixture in his neatly trimmed beard.

She couldn't read anything on Buzz's face. She turned and headed for the door to return home. The breeze was pleasant, and warm air rustled her skirt. Unease crept up her spine at the pending confrontation.

Back home, they readied for bed. Zara asked, "Darling, why did you say to Sebastian we were having a honeymoon? You know that's not anything we agreed to. Why can't you let us be us?"

Buzz looked so serious. "My darling Zara, I am done asking. We have been together for years. I'm committed to our relationship. I've supported you in every way I could. I want to marry you. Now. Today." He looked at her, trying to convey all the love in his heart. "I want to know that you're my wife. I want children with you. I want us to be a family like Mark and Marci are planning. I am done waiting." His breathing was labored from the outburst, but he continued, his voice a little louder and more insistent, "You turn me down every time I ask you to marry. Then you seduce me, thinking I'll forget the subject! You always say your bad past is why. I wasn't in your past. Should I try to guess why we'll have no marriage or family?"

Zara was unprepared for the emotions that overran her mind and body. She had kept her secret hidden for too long, and it would no longer be denied. "Buzz, I am not going to marry you. I have tried to keep you happily satisfied. But now, I, too, am done." She placed her hands on her hips and stood nearly nose to nose. "My early life was miserable. I told you I did many things I was not proud of and never wanted to repeat. I was in jail, but not the kind with bars made of steel. I was sold into service when I was twelve. For five horrific years, men rented me by the moment. I would never risk having a child to be subject to that type of life due to an unforeseen event. I can't be bound to a man who one day may think he can say what I can or cannot do." She raised her thickly accented voice. "I left that life when I decided I wouldn't remain a whore. I didn't want to tell you this secret, but it's out. Now I'm out too." She took a deep inhale. She was grateful he was speechless, as she continued, "You said you'd be happy with us. Our love never required a signed paper or a moment in front of the priest. We needed to work, play, and laugh together to thrive and grow." Her fatalistic tone was unmistakable. "You wouldn't take no for an answer, regardless of how often I said it. I am tired of repeating myself because I realize you'll never accept me for myself. I'm sorry love wasn't enough after all."

She stomped to the bedroom and took her worn suitcase from the closet. He followed but silently watched her, too numbed by what she'd announced. Zara packed her belongings. She retrieved her passport from the safe along with half the money. She added these items and some trinkets to her purse.

In a cold, distant way Buzz had never seen, Zara turned and stated, "I'm leaving. The university gig is yours. I have no claim. I wasn't enough for you. I can no longer endure this endless duel of telling you no, and trying to convey no doesn't mean I don't love you. I'll start over someplace else. Don't follow me. We owe each other nothing." She grabbed her bag and faced him again with a jut to her chin. "I wish you had listened for all these years so we could stay happy. Find someone else to build the family you need. It isn't me."

0 1 0 1 0 1 0 1 0 1 0 1 0 1 0

Zara turned and walked away quietly, shutting the door without a word. Thinking she would return shortly, he went to bed, hoping the entire exchange was a horrible dream. When morning arrived, and she wasn't by his side, tears gathered in his eyes.

He reluctantly rose and went to the kitchen for coffee. He sat stirring the sugar and realized it wasn't a dream. He operated in slow motion. Like a sledgehammer, it hit him that he'd pushed too hard for too long.

"She's smart," he mumbled. "I'll never find her unless she wants to be found. I failed to listen. What a fool I've been." He sat at the kitchen table, laid his head onto his folded arms, and wept. An hour later, he raised his eyes, staring into the bleakness of his future. "But I loved you so much, Zara. I wanted you to be with me forever, never to control you. I had no idea of your past. It means nothing to me. You are what counts." He inhaled and vowed, "I'll find you someday and tell you."

0 1 0 1 0 1 0 1 0 1 0 1 0

Buzz spent the next few days locked up in their apartment, missing work and ignoring calls. Early Thursday, incessant pounding on the door forced Buzz to react. Standing, he combed his hair with his fingertips and used his palms to wipe away the sleep from his eyes. He made his way to the door, barely noting the dirty dishes scattered on the tables, not recalling when he last ate.

"I'm coming," he shouted, wincing with pain as the sound exacerbated his headache. He yanked open the door. "You woke me, Sebastian. What's up?"

Sebastian pushed him aside, entered, and then stopped in the room. Turning to Buzz, he asked, "What in heaven's name happened? Where's Zara? I've been trying to reach you for days. Neither of you responded."

Buzz sank into the nearest chair and momentarily held his head in his hands. He took a breath. "Zara's, um, gone. I don't know where. We argued. She left. End of story."

Buzz focused his eyes enough to notice Sebastian picking up various cups and glasses. "What are you doing?"

Sebastian carried the dirty dishes to the sink and turned on the water. "This place is not how people should live." He grinned and thumbed his chest. "However, I am an organization expert, which extends to fixing almost anything." He pulled out a towel and tossed it to Buzz, who caught it. "I'll wash. You dry them and put them away. Then we'll talk."

Buzz stretched with each item he dried and put away. He felt things were out of control. Clean dishes wouldn't solve anything, and ignoring the mess worsened it.

Sebastian moved through the dishes like a professor grading papers, one at a time, in an orderly fashion. Sebastian wiped down the surfaces, inclining his head at the full trash can. "Take out the trash and replace the liner. Then go wash."

Buzz completed the task. With one look in the mirror, he decided a quick shower was in order. When he returned to the kitchen, he heard the gurgle of coffee brewing and the sounds of breakfast sizzling. He inhaled the smells of coffee and bacon.

Sebastian glanced at Buzz approvingly and pointed with the spatula, indicating that Buzz should sit. The table was set for two. Seconds later, Buzz's cup was filled with dark, strong coffee.

Two plates heaped with hash browns, bacon, and eggs were placed on the table as Sebastian took his place. "Eat. You look awful."

They took a few bites, Sebastian seeming to savor each bite. "What did you fight about?"

"I've been trying for years to marry her and pushed too hard. She's had it, and the recent overindulging in wine hasn't helped."

Sebastian shook his fork as he replied, "You have been drinking too much for the last month. But it's not that." He took another bite and chewed. "You two fit so well together. I need both of you to meet my commitment. What are you going to do about that?"

Buzz shook his head. "I don't know. I don't want to work without her."

"You don't have a choice. You signed the contract."

"I have some time off before the next semester, and I…"

"No, you don't. The last thing you need is to be alone. You and I will work together to reset the lab environment. I will insist that your temporary staff return on Monday. You will coordinate the training sessions. I'm counting on you."

Buzz tapped his chest with one hand. "Sebastian, my friend, my heart is broken. I miss her."

Sebastian reached over, patting Buzz's shoulder. "I know. She'll return. You two are good together. I've seen you. I've watched her look at you with tender expressions."

Buzz's eyes misted. "I don't think I can do as good a job."

"Eat up," he insisted. "I'm staying with you for a while. No drinking or feeling sorry for yourself. This is a temporary setback." He patted his stomach. "Healthy eating, exercise, and planning classes will help you focus. I'll help."

By Monday morning, Buzz felt physically better, but his heartache interrupted his sleeping with wild dreams. During breakfast, Buzz related one of his nightmares. The two men discussed women's fickle behavior and how much they enjoyed the sparring even as they tied their hearts in knots. Buzz realized he had a valuable friend in Sebastian. "Thank you, Professor. I needed a good swift kick in the butt."

Sebastian slapped his shoulder. "We all do, now and again. You've got this, el Señor Buzz."

Buzz struggled the first few days in directing the semester until he decided that keeping his teaching post was the best path. When she returned, he wanted to show her they could carve out a shared life. No more badgering about marriage. The only thing his heart and soul needed was Zara. It became his daily mantra.

Two and one-half weeks into the semester, warnings sounded for a significant tropical storm within 48 hours. Buzz marshaled his students to secure the infrastructure if they needed to provide communications again. The notices blossomed into a full-fledged hurricane that hammered Puerto Rico and was particularly harsh on San Juan citizens. Buildings fell. People were injured.

Everyone assisted the emergency response teams in the recovery of survivors. Buzz and his students established Internet connectivity with twenty-four-hour monitoring. In between visits to the lab, he worked to remove rubble, find victims, and hug friends who had lost loved ones.

One evening, Sebastian unexpectedly arrived with food. "One of the small shops reopened. Darci and Juan insisted I bring you food after you located Marco's puppy."

"That child hugged that puppy so close, I thought he might squash him." Buzz chuckled. "One of the bright spots in these bleak days."

"Everyone is raving about the support you provide. Thank you for the Internet connectivity; it's helping in so many ways. Who could have foreseen fifty years ago the value of technology."

Buzz smiled. "It is a wonder that keeps evolving. Which is why, my friend, your enrollment is increasing."

Sebastian nodded as he distributed their meal.

As he swallowed the last bite, Buzz said, "I still miss her. But I'm glad she wasn't in the middle of the destruction or worse."

"Things will work out, el Señor Buzz."

They both laughed. Buzz knew he appreciated the thanks from those community neighbors, taking his mind off the pain of losing Zara.

At sunrise, Buzz woke, determined to help the workers until his shift in the lab in the early afternoon. The operation lead assigned him a spot to remove debris. The mindless labor kept him distracted while he shoveled and moved fallen boards. A voice disrupted him.

"Lift with your legs, not your back. Back muscles are not designed to do the heavy lifting. Please, do it correctly. I wouldn't want you injured."

Buzz snapped his head around with stunned recognition.

Zara smirked and proclaimed, "I heard they needed help here. Mind if I pitch in? I kind of like this place."

"Ah…Zara?" he stuttered. "What are you doing here? Are you my imagination playing tricks?"

Zara laughed. "No, it's the real me. Don't look so surprised. Like all women, I changed my mind after thinking. I wanted to know you were safe when I saw the storm's destruction. However, if overly self-centered men can't…"

Buzz took a step and pressed his fingertips against her lips. "Hi, my name is Buzz. I missed you, pretty lady."

Zara caressed his sweaty face. "I'm looking for a man who knows my past but cares only about a future together. Can you recommend someone for that task?"

Buzz grinned. "I have several candidates, but they all look like me."

Zara laughed and hugged him. "You have confidence. I like that in a man."

"I'm sorry, Zara. I'm glad you came back."

"Me too. You know all the past. It was the hardest thing I ever told anyone."

He hugged her closer and whispered into her ear. "Let's enjoy being together, Zara."

The
Jewel

*H*addy recalled the harshness of the last two weeks, physically and mentally. Even at her young age and excellent health, the birth of her daughter was painful. They both survived, which was a good reason to give thanks. Sadly, reality sunk in as her beloved husband gingerly pushed the wheelchair with her and the newborn to the waiting sedan. Her melancholy reminded her of the devastating statement from the doctor.

"I'm sorry, Ma'am, but you can conceive no more children."

"I understand," she uttered, tears overfilling and trailing down her cheeks.

She looked at their new bundle of joy encircled in her arms and smiled. Her heart tore, knowing there would be no repeat performance based on the medical procedures conducted by the doctor. She was grateful that the love of her life, Otto, remained upbeat with her. Haddy knew he recognized the distant, forlorn look in her eyes because he told her he wanted a dozen children before they married.

This morning, Otto said, "Darling," as he brushed the blonde curls behind her ear, "I'm lucky to have you both ready to take home. We'll have a wonderful family. We have one perfect girl born of our love." Otto clasped her hand to his heart. "I know it'll take time for you to agree, but I vow I love you above all else."

"I am sad for you, Otto, with your desire for many children. I let you down."

"No, never, sweetheart. Don't despair, it is the us that is key to my heart. I love our daughter as much as you. Talk to me, darling, if you are sad."

Relief swept through her as Nadine, the newly hired au pair, met them at the sedan with a gentle smile. She planned to help Haddy into the spacious back seat of their Mercedes, complete with extra cushions and a soft cashmere blanket. Otto carefully gathered the sweet little bundle into his arms, who momentarily opened her huge blue eyes that matched those of her parents. They smiled, and Haddy kissed the baby's fingers.

Nadine assisted Haddy after she stood near the door. Nadine painstakingly arranged everything for comfort when the new mother slid into the car seat.

Settled, Haddy breathed and asked, "Let me hold her again, please." Her voice was choppy and conveyed her fear of doing anything wrong.

Dutifully, Otto gently passed the swaddled baby into Haddy's outstretched arms. "Thank you, she replied with a tear sliding down her cheek. "Otto, I don't deserve you or this precious bundle."

He patted her arm. "It will take time, darling, for you to realize it is I who doesn't deserve you. I'm by your side forever."

Otto realized time could heal the wounds and fears. Haddy could recover from the physical, as she was young and healthy, but the mental anguish was more challenging. He wanted to remind her not to mourn what was lost but to embrace what they gained. He was at a loss for how to convey his feelings. He realized if he forced anything too soon, she might lose her tentative hold on today and sink into an emotional puddle of despair.

On returning from work, Otto watched the interaction between mother and child in the evenings.

"Otto, Petra crawled across the library today. She looked at everything."

They both sat on the floor playing with their daughter, sharing all her milestones. Watching a child evolve is a wonder. He also watched the sadness pass across the face of his wife. "Darling, you look beautiful tonight," Otto said with a sweet kiss.

"Thank you, but I need to do more. She is so busy. I plan to let her swing tomorrow."

"Good. I will try to get home early so we can walk along the paths of our gardens."

Haddy nodded. Her smile didn't reach her eyes. Otto often pushed the carriage around the circle along. He began to fear for her emotional state.

The recovery gained ground over the next couple of years. Haddy masked her sadness but took joy in her child.

He returned home one evening, and Petra rushed for a hug. He picked her up and swirled her around.

"I see she likes dancing with her father," Haddy chuckled. "Perhaps I need to enroll her in dance class next year."

"Sweetheart, I agree. She's the spitting image of you with her lithe frame and blonde curls."

"Stop. She's perfect, whereas I am flawed. Our little Petra is sweet to her core and keeps me smiling. Today, she was reading from her books, and I think she's understanding the letters and words. She's smart like you, my love."

Otto watched Haddy's interaction with their daughter, clearly delighted with each milestone conquered. When Petra was three, Haddy insisted on a tea party table in the playroom with five settings. Two of the chairs contained stuffed animals. One was a brown bear wearing a yellow flowered dress made by Haddy, and the other was a doll with blond hair and a purple dress with a lace petticoat. Petra would sit and act as the hostess, with Haddy as a guest.

"Let me pour your tea, Ms. Bear," Petra offered. "You like two lumps of sugar and no cream."

Haddy clapped with approval and contributed silly small talk, but Otto noticed the shadow across her eyes when she looked at the empty chair. He didn't know how to fill the void that other children were meant to fill.

The days stretched into years, with Nadine helping shape their precious daughter.

"Otto," Haddy said one day, "Nadine is like family. I'm so glad she's stayed with us. When I feel melancholy, she ensures Petra has many activities."

"She is terrific, but mostly because of your great plans for our Petra, She's such a happy baby. I like having her at dinner trying to be so proper. And she's smart as a whip. She seems to like your idea of some days we speak Polish, others French, and one day a week of English."

Haddy nodded and smiled. "Her skills are improving and honestly helping me keep my skills. She needs playmates, but no one with children lives close to us."

He broached a sore subject, hoping the timing was right. "We could move closer to Ferdek. Petra enjoys his son Quip."

She flinched. "I'm sorry I failed us," she whispered. Wiping her mouth, she abruptly rose. He heard her cries as she left the table, knowing her bedroom door would be locked.

During the next few months, Otto noticed Petra's growth highlighted Haddy's sadness. More days were spent in bed,

which threatened not only her mental state but her relationship with Otto. Like a tightrope walker, Otto learned to
school his thoughts and comments to avoid aggravating her
emotionally bruised state. Their once-tight bond eroded as
Haddy avoided this sad topic.

On Haddy's birthday, to recapture their closeness, Otto
planned an exceptional adult evening out with dinner and
theater—just the two of them. Petra, aged four, would remain
with Nadine for the evening. Overcoming her resistance to the
outing with all the charm Otto possessed, they donned their
finery and headed out in the Bentley. Using all the polish of
the quintessential European gentleman, Otto escorted her
to the door, opened it with a flourish, and held her hand. A
little giggle erupted as he indiscreetly patted her fanny, which
lightened the mood—the evening promised renewal.

The dinner was splendid in their private corner of the candlelit
room. Fork-cut tender prime rib merged with the vintage
merlot. Otto and Haddy smiled and flirted with each other
like newlyweds through the warm, fragrant souffle. Otto saw
Haddy smile more than she had in years.

As he laughed at a story she was trying to relate to, it seemed
they turned the corner on this painful chapter of their lives.

Not wishing to interrupt the fun, they left a bit late for the
theater. The crowds slowed travel to the theatre. Otto grinned
because he'd selected such a popular show. Parking, even
with a valet service, was scarce. He took it upon himself to

park behind the adjacent building in the service alley. It was darker than he preferred, but with the play likely started, he refused to waste any more time driving around for a better spot. They were recapturing their special bond as a couple, and Otto refused to lose any of the evening's momentum. Before opening the door, he grabbed his walking cane for protection should action be required.

The luxuriously appointed silver Bentley did not escape the notice. It was magnified when Otto and Haddy stepped out of the car. Beautiful clothing and jewelry acted like beacons in the dimly lit service alley, silently shouting that these rich people were easy targets. Assumptions can be misconstrued.

The rough and uneven pavement of broken brick required them to step carefully to avoid a spill. Otto held Haddy's arm using the walking stick as intended. Thugs appeared from each side near the end of the service alley. One carried an iron pipe in his hand. They merged and then stood motionless in front of Otto and Haddy. The man slapped the tube to his empty palm to reinforce their menace. Though the thugs weren't big men, at six meters away, their attitudes and stench reeked of malice.

Otto released Haddy's arm and slowly moved in front of Haddy, who fearfully stepped back toward the car. Otto casually reached behind his back for the other end of the cane and withdrew the half-meter sword concealed inside. Holding the wooden sheath in his left hand and the sword in his right, he ensured the two thugs saw the dim light dancing off the blade. The one with the pipe appeared unimpressed and began to advance. The other thug held back, possibly thinking better of a confrontation.

Otto calmly asserted, "Gentlemen, I mean you no harm, but we're not the easy victims you hope. I'll not warn you again. Turn around and leave!"

The one with the pipe smirked and countered, "There's two of us. We want your money and jewels! We can do this the easy way or the hard way. Which way do you want to go?"

Otto chuckled. "That's what I was going to say!"

Otto wasted no time as he leaped to place a lunging frontal kick that caught the pipe-wielding thug squarely in the chest, sending him staggering backward into a dumpster. The other thug stood dumbfounded until he received a well-placed spin kick to the side of the head that sent him to the ground. The pipe-wielding thug tried to stagger to his feet, but Otto threw a hammering blow to the man's head, which sent the thug colliding with the dumpster and then to the ground. Otto positioning his sword to strike, stood to face the other man who'd gained his feet. The ruffian noted his disadvantage as he scrambled and took flight.

Haddy watched the drama unfold with wide eyes. With the odds even, Otto walked cautiously up to the stunned thug sprawled on the ground. Convinced his playing possum worked, the thug lunged forward only to have Otto drive his foot into the man's solar plexus. Otto succeeded by neutralizing the thug for good.

The fighting stopped. Haddy cautiously walked up behind Otto, who motioned her to stop. Haddy's attention wasn't on the incapacitated thug but focused on a faint mewing sound coming from inside the dumpster. Otto was still breathing hard as he gave Haddy a confused look, trying to understand why she was ignoring his caution. Then he, too, heard the sound. Otto verified that the thug remained unconscious and sheathed his sword. Together, he and Haddy looked for a way into the dumpster to locate the source of the sound. The metal dumpster appeared sealed all around with no discernable easy access.

Haddy's eyes grew large as he watched her panic rise.

She anxiously insisted, "That's a newborn cry. Otto, we've got to get into this dumpster and save the baby!"

A little unsure of the potential outcome of this scenario, Otto searched for access to the interior of the dumpster. He calmly suggested, "My darling, it could be a kitten mewing because it is stuck. It probably isn't…"

Haddy's eyes grew fierce with anger. "That's a human's cry. We're not ignoring it nor moving from here until we get this baby out. Do you hear me, Octavius?"

Otto continued to try to gain access as he quietly muttered, "The show is already half over, so why not do some dumpster diving?"

Finally, he shoved one of the metal panels on the front to the right with all his might. The rusty track moved and slid open for full access. They were astounded at what they found. Against the far wall of the dumpster, they discovered a carelessly placed cardboard box, half full of soiled swaddling clothes and a crying baby. Otto stood dumbfounded. When Otto intercepted her, Haddy was already on track to reach through the opening to retrieve the box or dive inside.

Without saying a word, he handed the cane to her and deftly swung in through the opening. After stumbling somewhat amongst the trash, he finally gained his footing and retrieved the baby. He gently handed the baby to Haddy through the opening, then swung himself out.

Haddy was frightened by what she saw and the condition of the baby. Her eyes were wild with terror as she demanded, "Otto, hospital, NOW!"

Once at the hospital emergency room, the staff went to work as if the baby was one of theirs. Otto explained the circumstances to the police and was obliged to return with the officers to the dumpster. They insisted upon a thorough inspection. Haddy refused to leave the baby's side. She calmly cooed and stroked a free hand, keeping out of the way of the staff.

The police investigation took longer than Otto would have liked. With an abandoned newborn, the authorities hunted for a local convent to take care of the baby. The police were familiar with a Mother Superior who helped with abandoned babies and might know the baby's mother. Haddy dug in her heels to stay with the infant despite the Mother Superior suggesting the convent could take care of the infant after the hospital released her.

Otto returned by the following morning to the hospital only to find that Haddy hadn't slept a wink during his absence. The ER staff pulled him aside and asked him to try and get her to go home. Her constant badgering for informational updates was becoming a big problem, even though she remained a calming factor for the sleeping baby.

Otto explained that the Mother Superior would arrive soon to take the baby, but Haddy ignored him. When he tried to convince her to go home, she angrily refused.

"I'm not leaving this little Jewel. Her mother already walked away and left her. I'm not going to let that happen again. I'll stay and explain this to the Mother Superior. You can leave. I'll find my way home!"

Fearful that Haddy was going over the emotional edge he'd been so worried about, Otto reminded her, "There is nothing more you can accomplish at this moment. We have our Petra at home, and she needs her mother. I'm worried about you needing rest. Let the ER staff do their work to monitor the baby and determine she's out of danger. You're coming home. Please don't worry; we'll return after you get some sleep."

Haddy began to crumble and sobbed. "We found her. Don't you understand? This little Jewel is our second child. We can care for her."

Otto held her as his tears joined with hers. He softly lamented, "This isn't our baby because we found her. Now come on home. Things will look different tomorrow. The baby will be here recovering."

Every day for a week, Haddy spent every waking moment at the hospital trying to help with the baby. She met with the Mother Superior and pleaded her case the first morning. One of the nurses took pity on Haddy and let her hold the baby, as it seemed to calm them both. No one seemed worried it might be a mistake to give Haddy false hope.

At the beginning of the second week, Mother Superior and Otto arrived at the hospital's nursery, where Haddy rocked the baby. As soon as Haddy saw Otto with the Mother Superior, her face went ashen.

Haddy railed, "You're here to take the baby away, aren't you? You brought Otto to help reason with me, didn't you? Well, you can't! We saved her, don't you understand? She's meant to be with us. I can't surrender her." Tears welled in her eyes. "Otto, please don't let her take my Jewel."

The Mother Superior looked at Haddy with kindness and patted her arm. "Madam, I've so many heartbreaking stories of people desperate to be parents, especially with the terrors of the war behind us. We keep lists of those willing to adopt or help foster the babies of young girls who have run scared, usually leaving the baby on our church steps. There may be another couple who requested help from the church. You and Otto aren't on our list. I understand you want her. I truly do. I'm forced to review our waiting parishioners."

Haddy began sobbing uncontrollably and haltingly implored, "Please no, not my little Jewel…not my little Jewel. She belongs to us…"

The Mother Superior looked sympathetic as she faced Otto. "Mr. Rancowski, can you explain it to her? I don't seem to be getting through."

Otto nodded and slowly stepped close to Haddy and touched her shoulder. "Sweetheart, after that close call with our first child, and based on what the doctor said, I've had our attorney working diligently to enter us onto adoption lists. We've applied everywhere and anywhere, but I've never told you because of what the Mother Superior just shared."

Otto thought back to the months of work he'd done to find alternatives to their adopting a child. The foundation of the church and community at large consisted of Kinder, Küche und Kirche, or Child, Kitchen, and Church. Haddy was aware of this framework.

"We're contributing members to the greater community. Since the war, we've helped our church rebuild with a stronger foundation in the three Ks. The bishop is aware and is lending guidance to help minimize our emotional and mental agitation with false hope. It's a curious twist of fate that we found a baby near this church where we are at the top of the lists in our church." Otto took a breath and smiled into the eyes of his bride. "Mother Superior wanted to be here when you learned that this little Jewel would come home with us because of our faith and commitment to family. We have our wish, my love."

Haddy almost collapsed from the emotional release that cascaded over her like a tsunami. Holding the baby close to her heart, she steadied herself against Otto. They both cried tears of joy as the Mother Superior said a prayer and blessed them before she turned to leave.

When he was finally able to command himself enough, Otto asked, "My love, what shall we call her? We now have the right to name her."

Not bothering to wipe away her tears, Haddy proudly proclaimed, "We found our Jewel, " which means her name should be Julie. Julie, my little Jewel."

The three of them went home shortly after the discussion. It was like a cloud moved, and the sun shone with hope and love. Petra assumed her role as the big sister the moment she saw Julie.

"Mama, I vow I'll protect her!"

Haddy replied, "I knew you would, Petra. Thank you for being such a wonderful daughter. I love you. You and your new sister will have so much fun together. With you, our Jewel will have a perfect model to follow. You can help her learn so many things."

"Yes, Mama. It will be wonderful. May I read her a story?"

Haddy sat comfortably in the cushioned leather chair. She was instantly pulled from her memories to the present, with the noisy steps of her two favorite children running across the hardwood floors. Juan Jr and Gracie squealed with delight and announced, using their outside voices, "Grandma, Mama's here! Mama's here!"

Haddy recognized the sensation of an escaped happy tear on her cheek as she bent to hug them. Looking up, she discovered Julie smiling at her.

"Daydreaming again, I see," her daughter commented, "Was it a good one?"

Not bothering to wipe the tear, she patted Julie's hand and smiled as she confessed, "It was a jewel, my darling."

Hot
Chocolate

*P*etra hummed to the music from the stereo while admiring the red, orange, and yellow flames dancing in the fireplace with random snaps and crackles. Recalling another store to call for a reservation, she added it to her growing list of things to do. Shifting to tuck her legs beside her on the sofa, she spotted the big flakes falling outside the window; she grinned, realizing December often rolled out a fresh blanket of snow. She and Jacob adored the holiday season in *Zürich*, blending their childhood traditions for the holidays. The celebration became even more choreographed during the five years since John Wolfgang was born. Christmas morning was for spoiling, while the rest of the season explored other cherished traditions. They worked to ensure JW, as they nicknamed him unless he was in trouble, experienced both the European and American season practices. It made seasonal celebrations more theirs as a family.

They made a pact to only travel for work during Christmas if an emergency arose with a customer. They were increasingly adept at handling remote support for customers as the family's technology capabilities increased. It had worked for all but one year. Even then, she had arrived home minutes before Christmas ended with the news that JW was on the way. The gift was outstanding, and they adored their son.

Every year since they found one another, she left no stone unturned to find the unexpected gift for the man she loved. The weeks of playful insanity were worth it on Christmas as they would laugh, enjoy the selections, and reaffirm their love. However, this year, she was pondering on what to give Jacob when she heard him walk out of JW's room, and he slid onto the sofa beside her "JW fell asleep before the end," he commented, "so I'm sure I'll read *The Little Engine That Could* again tomorrow."

Petra chuckled. "We're going on two weeks with that one. He likes the voices you do."

"I know. We must find a new Christmas book during our upcoming holiday adventures." He laid his arm over her shoulders and smiled. I've found the perfect Christmas surprise for you. You'll love it!"

She rubbed her hands together and grinned. "Lucky you, already finished shopping. You're going to be an incessant tease, I bet."

He tilted her chin with two fingers, looked into her eyes, and said in the tenor voice that made her giddy, "Oh, still shopping, huh?" he chuckled and added a quick kiss. "We have days and days until Christmas evening. You probably have something already squirreled away."

"You never know, do you?" She patted his hand.

"Exactly, that's why I love our secret challenge. Thanks, honey, for supporting my crazy ideas. As an only child in New York City, my mom worked hard to make the holidays multi-national flavored. Seeing the annual Macy's parade and finding surprises in the stocking hung by the fireplace was special for me. Christmas evening with just us and our gift exchange is something I look forward to every year."

She patted his thigh and leaned in. "We get to have fun and enjoy the holidays through the eyes of a child." Sighing, she added, "JW is like a gift every day."

"You're right, and it will be a whole different fun this year."

"Exactly. This year, we're focusing on all the activities based in Switzerland, building upon the traditions you and I have created since marriage. Non-stop action from November until New Year's Day. We have some dinners, family events, and a couple of trips. Everything is reserved to ensure smooth sailing. I think he's going to love it."

"Do we get to do some decorating and cooking here, or are we gone the whole time."

"No, sweetheart, we'll be here some in between delightful jaunts."

"I'm up for family fun and relaxation." He leaned over and started tickling her until she begged for mercy.

"Stop, stop, Jacob," she begged, wishing he too were ticklish. "I'm tired, honey, and ready for bed." She held him tight. "Tomorrow, we must pack early for the first trek featuring all the winter sports. I know you'll help teach our little guy to optimize his balance like all kids in the snow."

"You're right. I'll fix breakfast and let you sleep in. Then we pack."

Petra was pleased with the extra half-hour sleep and awakened to the smell of cinnamon rolls. She stretched and completed her morning rituals before dashing downstairs for her share of sweets.

She heard her guys talking low as she rounded the doorway.

"Good morning, Mama, we got rolls and eggs all ready for you," JW beamed, waving his hands at the plates on the table.

She tousled his hair, kissed Jacob on the cheek, then slid into her chair. "Thank you both. This looks delicious and smells inviting." Filling her plate, buttering the warm pastry increased her appetite. Jacob set a cup of tea by her place, and she flashed a smile. "Thank you."

"Of course. What's our plan for today, honey?"

"After breakfast, I'll do the dishes since you cooked. I would like you to help JW with his packing. Since we plan four days, he'll need six changes if he rolls in the snow and gets soaked. Then you can load up the snowboard, skis equipment, and ice skates, please."

JW started jumping in his seat with delight. "Oh, boy, I get to go with you? May I be excused so we can get started."

Jacob chuckled. "We decided it was a great time to have you practice winter sports. Mommy found this great location and rented some equipment for you to use. Since you're growing so fast, we decided not to buy yours yet." JW twisted in his seat, itching to get excused but waiting for permission. Petra saw the twinkle in Jacob's eyes. "Oh yes, you can be excused."

Petra chuckled when JW popped to the floor and started jumping up and down by Jacob's chair, tugging on his hand.

"Dad, we need to do what Mommy said. I can help."

Petra rose and began clearing the table. "Have fun, guys."

"Let's go, buddy."

She finished the dishes and wiped the counters. Seeing everything in order, she returned to their bedroom to pack their bags.

They loaded for the drive to St. Moritz shortly before noon. Jacob maneuvered their four-wheel drive SUV smoothly onto the main road toward their destination.

"Let's see how many shapes we can find in the clouds," suggested Petra. She stared at the blue sky with scattered white clumps resembling whipped cream for a moment, then returned her attention to her son.

JW pointed and squealed, "I see two dogs wrestling for a bone."

"I see it, too," Jacob commented after he glanced out the side window.

"Good one, JW," Petra agreed, "That's two points for you. Can you see the mama bear holding her cub?"

"Yes," he shrieked. "Ooo, it's changing to a lion."

The winding road showed evidence of vegetation asleep for the winter. Blue, brown, and black shades defined the mountain crevices that peeked through the snow. The white blanket appears thick in spots like scoops of ice cream plopped over the dramatic hillsides.

They played for an hour until the mountains prevented visibility to the sky. Petra switched to singing their favorite songs, which they all joined in. Then, she outlined all the tricks they could learn while ice skating until they pulled into the hotel's entrance, which was charmingly decorated for the holidays. They quickly checked in. JW asked non-stop questions they both answered in turn.

They made short work of organizing the room and putting things away. Their room had a large picture window displaying the endless possibilities in this winter wonderland. Looking out their hotel window, Petra suggested, "Jacob, look! I believe the snow is inviting you to snowboard."

Jacob and JW rushed to the window. "Sweetheart, you're right. That drift by the trees looks like a beckoning hand."

Wide-eyed, JW vigorously nodded. "I see it. Can I go snow-boarding too, Mommy?"

Petra knelt and grinned, looking into the same glacier-blue eyes as her husband. He was a younger version of her drop-dead gorgeous husband. "I thought you and I would ice skate. You can perform for Daddy when he gets done surfing the snow."

She delivered a stern set toward Jacob and taunted, "Remember, no trees this time."

Jacob refused to take the bait, suggesting he had crashed into the woods and picked up his board. He stood it on end next to his son and twirled it like a top. "Remember, JW, you must be taller to control a snowboard. I'll teach you when you get bigger."

Looking at his parents, he grinned. "Yes, sir! I am growing like crazy, according to the lines on the wall at home. Maybe next year.

"Mommy, you will teach me all the tricks we discussed, right?"

"Yes, honey. Unpack, get dressed for skating, and wear two pairs of socks. It's you and me, buddy."

While JW dashed away to complete his tasks, Petra rose and encircled her husband in a sweet embrace. Extending onto her tiptoes, she whispered, "Darling, you're going to be so surprised this year. I found that note from your secret wish list."

She kissed him soundly, grinned, and strutted away to unpack her things. The mirror reflected a shift in his facial expression with one raised eyebrow. She hoped he wondered if she looked at his list of most wanted items stashed on his laptop. Even password-protected, she could open it if she tried. She hid her grin behind her hand when it seemed to dawn on him that she played him like a master telemarketer.

Ready to enjoy the winter sports of the resort, they departed their room minutes later. JW babbled excitedly about everything he would learn. They reached the lobby as he loudly promised, "I bet I'll be an Olympic contender by the end of the day!"

Petra and Jacob laughed while other guests chuckled at the enthusiastic child.

Petra leaned into Jacob. "Please take care, honey," she whispered concernedly. "I want to watch you when you are warmed up, not help tend wounds."

He laughed. "I'll be ready to show you both." He crossed his heart. "And I promise I won't do any wood chopping with the snowboard." He kissed her cheek, then patted his son's back. "JW, you take care of your mommy. I'll find you at the rink in a few hours, ready to watch what you've learned."

Jacob's lips felt like butterfly wings as he whispered in her ear, "You need to stay safe, my love, so you can enjoy unwrapping what I have for you this year."

Petra chuckled. "We'll see, darling, if it is as good as the one you get to open."

JW perked up. "What are you talking about, Mommy? Open what?"

"Nothing, my darling son. Daddy and I are just being silly.

"Let's go!"

Petra steeled her expression to hide her angst. She hadn't decided on the present for Jacob. No time now to shop. Jacob liked playing this game, but he never bluffed about their gifts. Their banter was part of escalating the anticipation. He never showed disappointment; rather, he behaved like a five-year-old with his first bicycle with every gift each year. She considered looking at his laptop, but that was his space, and she respected his privacy. The point was the creativity and thoughtfulness, not spending a certain amount.

Jacob hugged them both as he took off for his daredevil fun. Petra and JW put on their skates, fortunate to be the only people using the rink. JW illustrated his natural balance and athletic ability within the first fifteen minutes while holding her hand. With all the gusto of a gazelle, he was off like a shot, lapping her along the outside edge. He pulled up next to her and skidded to a stop, throwing up a layer of ice spray to match his gleeful laugh.

"I think I'm doing good, Mommy, don't you?"

"You have the basics mastered, including stopping with style. Let's try some figures."

Petra, an accomplished skater, started with simple figure eights. JW intently watched her steps. He traced the path she etched in the ice, first with one foot, then the other. Petra smiled at his focus and mimicking ability. JW did the same with every subject, like reading and even the gaming program development Jacob taught him. No fear, hesitancy, or barriers to moving forward for this child. They added a simple jump and land, then switched to moving backward. He mastered it as Jacob arrived at the ice's edge carrying a tray of steaming drinks. Moving closer, she caught the faint scent of her favorite cocoa beverage.

JW spotted him and raced to the side, turning just in time to send a spray of beautiful crystals onto Jacob's legs.

"Impressive, JW. Very controlled. Do you want to show me what you learned or take a break?" He nodded toward the covered cups he held.

JW beamed. "Daddy, is that hot chocolate, I hope?"

"Yes, it is, or it used to be until you showered it with ice."

"The steam makes it appear super-hot. Let me show you what I learned, and then I'll take a break."

Without waiting for a response, he rushed off for the center of the ice. Petra undid her skates, slid on her boots, and leaned against Jacob as they focused on JW. He started by speeding around the area several times, teetering on the edge of his skates, nearly falling but maintaining his balance. JW performed a couple of modest jumps before returning to them with a string of figure eights, then gently stopping this time for a bow. It made Petra and Jacob laugh when his skates slid out from under him, leaving him sitting on the ice.

The rosy cheeks and big eyes highlighted his broad grin of success. "That's it." He trusted out his arms like a master showman. "I'll learn to make higher jumps with practice or when I am taller like you, Daddy. May I take off my skates and have my hot chocolate now?"

Petra took the tray, and Jacob swooped JW into his arms as they retreated to a nearby table to relax. JW and Jacob's similarities in bone structure, mannerisms, and energy never ceased to amaze Petra. While sipping, they planned the rest of their time at the resort. More skating and snowboarding time topped the list of activities. Petra was confused about why Jacob could not tempt JW to try skiing. After eating a fabulous meal, they retired to their suite. They all were sound asleep as their heads melted into their pillows.

Jacob woke to the sounds of the shower running and JW staring at him. "Mommy sent you a text and told me not to look, so I didn't. After she finishes, we need to get ready to go out."

"Sounds good!" Jacob's fingers combed JW's hair as he read the text.

You are going to love Christmas night, honey!

Jacob snickered. "JW, let's get ready. One pair of socks is cool since we aren't skating."

"Yes, sir."

Jacob observed as JW carefully extracted the clothes he wanted. When he was a kid, his drawers were always a jumble. Petra was the organizer. He finished dressing as Petra appeared moments later dressed for the day, with a bloom in her cheeks.

"Good morning!" She kissed them both and hurried them out the door. "Come on, guys, I'm famished."

After breakfast, they met up with Ben, their assigned guide, and his dog, provided by the resort. JW loved overseeing the St. Bernard as they took the long hiking circuit. Ben explained landmarks and various points of interest. Jacob caught a bunch of candid shots on his phone.

JW petted and hugged the dog whenever possible. He started a conversation with their chaperon, Ben, making Jacob silently chuckle.

"Mr. Ben, how long have you had Bo, the most wonderful furball I've ever touched?"

"Almost ten years. He's a good boy."

"He's wonderful. But isn't it time he stopped working? I could take care of him for you."

"I don't know, son, I'm fond of Bo. He keeps me company."

"I can understand that. I love him and want to walk him, brush his coat, and feed him. He could sleep by my bed."

"Son, that's a fine offer, thank you. But I would be lonely without Bo."

He patted Ben's arm. "Oh, I wouldn't want that. If you get tired of him, call my dad, and we'll come get him."

They all laughed. The day was delightfully filled with fun activities, humorous conversations, and another great sleep.

The last morning in St. Moritz, the three of them piled into the horse-drawn sleigh to ride through the shimmering snow-blanketed mountains. This trip was a photographer's bonanza. The sun bounced off the glistening landscape, creating images they discussed at length.

Jacob's breath looked like crystalized fog as he said, "This is better than playing cloud art while hiking. After we get home, let's load up these photos and try to find the hidden images to outline. The mountains are breathtaking."

They enjoyed several outings from their home base in Switzerland over the next few weeks. Going to the chocolate factories to sample this year's creations topped the must-do list. Jacob appreciated Petra's passion for rich, creamy Swiss chocolate requiring plenty of samples to come home for months of enjoyment. The molds, decorating, and fillings were works of art.

Jacob loved watching Petra as she picked hostess gifts for the seasonal dinners they planned to attend. He spotted a few smuggled pieces she had shopkeepers privately reserve as a part of their purchases. He suspected these might be included in JW's stocking on Christmas morning.

Jacob teased, "Thank goodness the cold winter temperatures will keep the chocolate from melting while you hug the bags so close."

While JW perused every shop window, adding a running commentary on every item that caught his fancy, they moved toward the next destination.

Jacob leaned into Petra and conspired, "No matter what, we aren't doing another hide-and-seek game following the chocolate clues like we did that year. Oh, yeah! That gift continued giving when the ants found the one missing piece in the spring. You were so mad."

"I was, honey." She feigned a frown, then placed her hand on her forehead and dramatically said, "Good chocolate gone to waste. Some things are worth repeating, and the map must mark all the spots."

They laughed. Holding hands, they kept an eye on their curious boy who was onto the next shop.

JW had learned about hot chocolate at the age of three. It was one item he researched passionately when he first learned about the power of computer searching. He saw no reason to refuse a chance to sample whenever possible. Then, he'd thoughtfully offer his opinion on each version of the preferred drink of the angels. Shopkeepers loved his detailed breakdown of their variance on the popular beverage. He was respectful while delivering both the merits and criticisms of their efforts. This year, he was much more detailed as his vocabulary and knowledge of cocoa history had grown. Delighted, enthralled shopkeepers laughed along, complimenting Petra and Jacob on their delightful child. JW's honesty earned him more than one bit of the high-end cacao bean creations to complement the warm beverages.

Only a week remained until Christmas, and Petra had yet to find Jacob a gift. Each day, they teased each other more, his quite serious and hers more bravado. The anxiety level went up a notch each time she noticed how fast time was fleeting and her options dwindling. Shipping in anything on time was not happening, so she needed to find something closer to home.

In desperation, she phoned her sister. "Jules, I'm frantic. I've nothing for Jacob. I get so distracted by everything, but nothing says buy this for Jacob."

"Sis, you're being too hard on yourself. You have a lot going on. How many events have you orchestrated for your boys so far? That's like a gift in itself." Julie laughed, "My twins would be delighted if I'd created so many memories in one holiday season. How about the shop in town that has models in a box? Jacob enjoys sailing, and they have those tall ships. He could craft one, and you could enclose tickets for a trip next year. Or, perhaps you could get him and Juan tickets to the international soccer games; I'd split the cost. The added benefit here is we get time together."

"I love you. I envy your easy relationship with Juan. Your ideas are interesting, but we need a romantic flare."

"Like a poem or a song dedicated to him. Or heck, create a night to remember, and I'll keep JW."

"I'm too tired for that. With all the activities, I'm falling to bed and sleeping like a rock. Not too much romance these days. I'll keep working on it."

"All right. Sorry I couldn't give you the perfect idea."

"I'll figure something out. Talk tomorrow."

This week, the Nutcracker performance was first on the list. JW loved the story and the music. She and Jacob loved how he embraced the holidays wholeheartedly and appreciated his youthful vantage point. This show promised to be the perfect cure for humdrum. Petra researched locally handcrafted nutcrackers, finding a couple of examples different and unique enough that she added these to the list of maybes for Jacob.

Their train ride to Mt. Jungfraujoch two days later was more thrilling than Petra recalled from her childhood. The trip featured seasonal decorations and storytelling along the route. JW clung to Jacob the whole way, chattering like a magpie as he pointed out everything discussed by the conductor. The increase in youthful passengers made the conductors grow more animated and engaged with their travelers.

Though they had decorated the house at the beginning of December, the greenery and seasonal flowers changed weekly. The expansive living room provided the perfect setting for the Christmas tree, with lots of seating, windows, and a fireplace that kept the room cozy.

Tree trimming began early on Christmas Eve, unloading several boxes of decorations, lasting until dinner. Morning hugs and kisses began the process. Jacob helped Petra carry sweet rolls and beverages to the table within easy reach. She opened the first box, lifting a small tissue-packed item. She unwrapped it, grinning at the small nutcracker before placing it on a bow. Wringing her hands, she was distracted by this and that.

"Are you okay?" Jacob asked.

"Yes. How about you and JW do the tree while I care for the other items on my list?"

His brow furrowed like he was concerned. "What things are you planning, and can I help? You're looking a little stressed."

She flashed him a smile and gave him a quick kiss. "It's all good. We are hosting dinner tomorrow, and I want to make a few dishes today. You know a few friends might drop by, so I wanted to prepare some trays just in case." Nodding, she added, "And a few last-minute wrappings."

JW interrupted the conversation by grabbing a golden star ornament from the box and carefully removing the paper. He made them laugh, reciting the item's history and when he'd first seen it.

The guys became the primary decorators, seriously discussing placing various items. Side by side, there was no mistaking their resemblance. She smiled and wandered between rooms, knocking things off her list.

Petra hummed along with the seasonal music. Nutmeg, cinnamon, allspice, and roasting meat aromas filled the air as she prepared different dishes. Periodically, she complimented their efforts or paused to listen to JW's memory of various items.

Midday, Petra received an incoming call from her sister. "Hi, Jules, what's up?" She listened for a bit, then smiled. "Jocab, I need to finish this discussion in the other room," Petra said, rolling her eyes. "Keep him busy, honey. I know you two can finish the tree. It looks great, and JW is having so much fun."

"Mommy, this is the best time of the year. Do I still get a special present if I'm extra good?"

A thoughtful smile played on Jacob's lips. "Don't Mommy and I give you a special present every year, JW? How about we surprise her by finishing the tree before we stop for a late lunch?"

"Mommy, don't you want to help decorate?"

"I can't right now. I need to finish this call with Aunt Julie. You know how she can talk."

Jacob stood back and admired their handiwork after Petra left the room. The lights glowed on the branches of the long-needled pine, looking lovely and reflecting on the shiny surfaces of the decorations. He recalled they tried using candles the year before JW arrived. Petra said no more, citing children did not need the temptation of candles until they got older. Jacob agreed but loved the old-world tradition and was grateful they had pictures.

Once all the decorations were perfect, he smiled.

"Son, grab the topper, please?"

JW rushed to pick up the last item and reverently stroked the golden hair of the angel. Jacob hoisted the child onto his shoulders. "All right, this is it."

He watched the giggling lad carefully place the prized tree topper, then swooped his son to the ground. They fist-bumped and then looked up in awe. JW rushed to turn off regular lights so they could enjoy the tree as it glowed with the rainbow of colors.

Jacob noticed as Petra watched from the doorway as they judged their handy work from different angles. He figured she was happy as she approached, a little teary-eyed, and wrapped him in a hug.

"Even though it's smaller than you wanted, watching you guys fills my heart with love and unmatched pleasure. JW, the tree is stunning. I'm glad you finished it. Thank you. Aunt Julie reminded me of the two items I require for tomorrow's roast from my mom's recipe. I forgot to add them to the shopping list. I called, and the store in town has the items. I need to go grab them before they close."

"Honey, I can run to the store if it's easier for you," Jacob offered.

Petra smiled. "No, thank you. You boys are on a roll. The last box has some of the extra mantle items if you want more to do. I'll go and be back in a flash to help. I just wanted you to know I was leaving." She bent her knees to get eye-level with JW and embraced him before her lips moved into a sly smile.

"By the way, did you happen to smell the cookies I baked earlier?"

JW nodded vigorously.

"I put a couple of sandwiches in the refrigerator and cookies on the counter that should be cool if you get hungry."

Her cheeks were a little flushed. Jacob rose and walked over, pulling her into an embrace. "Are you feeling alright? You seem a bit off."

"I'm fine. You know how I get annoyed with myself when I forget things? I'll be back shortly. Promise." She kissed him and then left the room.

It seemed like a good time for a break. Jacob and JW fetched the items and a pot of hot chocolate to the coffee table to snack on while they worked. Returning to the task at hand, Jacob handed the last box to JW, reminding him to carefully open it. Before they had gotten very far, the house phone rang. As the self-appointed phone call greeter, JW ran to answer it.

"Michaels' residence, JW speaking." After a few pleasantries, JW brightly offered the phone to Jacob. "It's my funny uncle, Daddy."

Jacob brightened. "Hi, Quip. What's up?"

"I'm known as the *funny uncle* at your house. Does that mean Eilla-Zan is the *funny aunt*? I was calling to have you help cheer me up."

Jacob thought Quip's tone sounded amused.

"Cheer you up, Quip? You're always on top of the world with no worries. Why, suddenly, do you need cheering up?"

"EZ thinks she might be pregnant. That puts her in charge again. Remember how crazy she was when carrying Granger? I now get to make Christmas dinner instead of her, though she'll offer suggestions."

"Quip, old friend, she's always in charge."

He sniggered. "True, but EZ is on the phone with Julie and maybe Petra. I wanted you to have a heads-up. This Christmas thing is so…emotionally challenging all by itself. Granger is a non-stop talker who knows everything. I don't know where he gets that attitude. It must be EZ, right?"

"Possibly. JW has been chatting all day, but we finished the tree." He winked at his son, who was eating his sandwich, but gave a thumbs-up response.

"Now it's baby planning time again," Quip groused. "We're working on name lists after Granger goes to bed tonight. She hasn't seen a doctor yet or taken a do-it-yourself home test. She says she just knows."

Jacob swallowed. He and Petra resigned themselves to having only JW. He found himself a little jealous and sad that his wife had been unable to conceive. "Quip, that's great. I know you'll be delighted if she's right. You lucked into a great partner, so don't complain. After the first of the year, she can get the doctor's opinion. Congrats to you both. I promise I'll be surprised when Petra tells me, or wait for EZ, whichever they decide. You know how girls are about secrets; no sooner done than said. How do you feel about another baby in your midst?"

Chuckling, Quip replied, "A baby is terrific if EZ is happy. She does most of the work, you know. If she's right, then my work is done! And you're right. They'll have so much fun and distraction for months until the baby arrives. Cheers, Jacob! Merry Christmas. I think I'm going to play with the baby's mother. Talk later."

Not willing to let his good friend off that easy, Jacob added, "Same to you, Quip. Just think…it might be twins."

Quip sputtered. Smiling, Jacob disconnected the phone and found his son staring at him

"Daddy, what is twins? Can I look it up if I need to."

Jacob replied, "Twins are where something matches, like your cousins. Juan and Gracie are twins because they were born on the same day."

Satisfied, JW returned to unwrapping the mantel decorations and settling them in the open spaces. Jacob helped arrange the taller items to the back so everything could be seen. They had a rhythm to their efforts. Jacob changed music channels to one JW liked.

Jacob grinned, believing Petra would return excitedly with the news of EZ. He only hoped she wouldn't be sad. Last year, they agreed to pursue adopting this coming January. Jacob hoped the options he collected to review with her after the holidays would please her. After all, Julie was her adopted sister and best friend, which worked out perfectly.

Petra returned with a spring in her step and a couple of bags in her hands. "Wow, you two were busy. The decorations appear nearly finished. Let me put the groceries away, and I'll be right back to help if there's anything left to do."

Jacob offered, "I'll put those away if you want to sit down and relax."

Petra's eyes twinkled with eagerness. "It'll only take a few minutes; I'll be right back. JW, save at least one decoration for me, okay?" JW nodded, bouncing around and looking at everything with wide-eyed wonder.

"Jacob, did Quip call you?" she asked with a mischievous smile. "I made a bet with EZ that he did and that you already know."

He nearly choked on the swallow of his cocoa, realizing he'd been made. "Yes, and yes. Great news, isn't it?"

Turning toward the kitchen, she looked over her shoulder and commented, "It is wonderful. She's so happy even though she must do the formal test at the end of next month."

JW cocked his head and looked concerned. "Daddy, does EZ have to take a formal test? I didn't know she was in school."

Chuckling at the levels of conversation and realizing little would get by JW, Jacob made a mental note to speak to his lovely wife about this.

"Aunt EZ needs to go to the doctor for a test next year. You know how, near your birthday, you go to the doctor for some tests or an annual shot. Adults do that, too. That's all."

"Yes, but I'm not a fan of the shots," JW affirmed.

"Me either, buddy."

Jacob turned to Petra. "Sweetheart, you look fabulous. I think a little girl time did you good. We're ready for you to finish off this masterpiece. Are you finished cooking, though? I thought you had to get some ingredients."

Looking quite smug, she responded, "I added them. The concoction will finish marinating by morning. It will be a perfect Christmas meal."

Petra took her assigned items and placed them thoughtfully on the mantel. She stepped back to admire the results.

JW clapped and jumped around. "Mommy, it's perfect now. Let's have another cup of hot chocolate and tell stories."

Jacob took his cue and went to the kitchen to retrieve some cocoa, eggnog, and a plate of cheese and crackers with fruit for snacking. He set down the tray for easy access, then added more logs to the fire. The lights were off, but the golden glow brightened the entire room. JW found the stack of famed Christmas stories and chose his favorite. JW faced the fire, snuggled close to Jacob, and opened the book.

JW cleared his throat. "'Twas the night before Christmas, when all through the house."

Jacob draped his arm over Petra's shoulder and pulled her close, whispering, "Just one more night until your perfect gift."

"Uh-huh, and one more night until yours. Now, shhh, I want to hear our son." Petra leaned into his shoulder, feeling contented.

They each read a story aloud, setting the mood for a peaceful sleep.

JW fixed a small plate of reindeer treats, setting them near the side of the fireplace opening. He raced to hug and kiss his mommy. The embers were glowing a soft red. Jacob offered JW a piggyback ride to bed.

The two of them laughed and giggled, going upstairs to bed. Petra took out the stockings she had filled yesterday morning that were hidden in the cabinet. She double-checked with a practiced eye that the contents were intact and hung them on their designated hooks on the mantel. Then, she went to the cubby under the stairs to retrieve the modest number of gifts. Before turning out the lights, she looked at the idyllic scene she thought Pieter Bruegel the Elder would applaud.

Petra heard Jacob talking to JW on her way to their bedroom, recognizing their goodnight routine would soon end. She rushed to complete her nightly rituals. Petra slid into bed, selecting her latest cozy mystery novel from the side table to read while she waited for Jacob. She drifted off to sleep, sensing the lights were off. The movement of the mattress wasn't enough to end her twilight journey to rest. Petra heard Jacob murmur in her dream, "You are the best part of our family, my love. Our family is perfect as long as we're together."

Jacob awoke to sunrise, filling the room with light. He grinned, realizing Christmas had arrived. He dressed and straightened the room, figuring his lovely bride was already working on food. Sneaking a look outside the door to verify no one was around, Jacob rushed to his side of the closet and pulled out the wrapped gift hidden in his travel bag. He had the local jeweler create this custom piece. He hoped Petra would be surprised. Re-hiding the present on his nightstand, he covered it with his current mystery novel.

Upon seeing Jacob atop the stairs, JW yipped, "Daddy, Daddy, come on. The stockings are here." His energy was contagious.

"Stockings. No, son, they're on my feet. I can show you," Jacob teased.

Looking appalled, JW lamented, "Not that kind of stocking. It's Christmas, Daddy. You know, stockings hung up." He stomped his foot to emphasize his impatience. "Please, they're waiting for you to come downstairs. Mommy won't let me touch them until you arrive."

JW scrambled upstairs, grabbing Jaccob's hand to shepherd him.

"Good morning, Daddy. Merry Christmas." Louder still, JW announced, "Mommy, daddy's up. Come on, let's do stockings, please."

Petra giggled from the kitchen. She appeared moments later with a towel, wiping her hands. "Did you need something, JW? Good morning and Merry Christmas, Jacob. He thought you'd never wake up."

Jacob found coffee in the pot on the serving cart and poured it, inhaling the awakening fragrance of dark roast. Taking a sip, he said, "Merry Christmas. Let's do this!"

JW dutifully fetched his mommy's stocking and brought it to her. "St. Nick must have thought you were good. This stocking's heavy." He scampered back to get Jacob's, presenting it with similar commentary. Then he rushed back to retrieve his own. "Wow, I think mine is the heaviest."

Their stockings included a game, wrapped gifts, dried fruit in individual tins, loose nuts, and some coins to donate to church that morning. They admired the goodies and opened the few presents under the tree, resulting in hugs.

After completing a modest breakfast, they left for morning services. As they entered, friends greeted one another as each sat in their family pew. The service lifted spirits throughout the entire congregation. Jacob led Petra and JW out, stopping now and again for short greetings. Petra extended invitations to several families to join them during the day for a bite to eat along with holiday cheer. An open house was a tradition Petra and Jacob cultivated.

The afternoon included a steady stream of visitors. JW entertained the children while their parents enjoyed the delicious food, gay conversation, and catching up on all the news. Jacob and Petra were gracious hosts, making sure their guests enjoyed themselves. As the afternoon waned and the guests left, JW was losing steam.

"Honey, I'll take care of the dishes," Petra offered. "After all your marvelous preparation, it's the least I can do. JW would love having you tuck him in."

Petra handheld the tired boy upstairs. She was pleased that he scrubbed his teeth, washed his face and hands, then loudly yawned. She picked him up, and he nestled into her shoulder and murmured, "Mommy, it was such a nice day. I adored my Christmas gifts. Thank you for everything. I love you and Daddy this much." He gripped her neck in a delightful squeeze.

"You made it the bestest day for us. We love you, JW." Petra kissed her son on the forehead, gently touched his cheek with her fingertips, and tucked him under the covers. The door closed without a sound as she left.

Rushing to her bedroom, she showered and primped for Christmas night, sliding into the lavender silk robe Jacob adored. She leaned against the sofa cushions under a soft woolen blanket, her toes stretching to capture the heat from the low burning fire.

"Don't you look lovely," Jacob commented before kneeling and slowly kissing her. "Are you ready for our Christmas, sweetheart?"

"Go take your shower. I'll be right here."

She heard noise indicating he wasted no time in his evening regimen. The drawer of his nightstand slid open with its unmistakable sound. He slid in beside her, warm from his shower. He held her close. "I forget. Who's turn is it to go first, my love?"

Petra lifted her chin to gaze into his beautiful eyes, offered a come-hither smile, and replied, "It's always ladies first, honey. How many times do I need to tell you?"

He placed the package onto her palm as she extended her hand. She turned and looked at the wrapping from every angle. It was perfect. Either he wrapped it several times, or a shop did it. She shook it but heard nothing. Carefully, she untied the bow and peeled the tape off the paper. She saw him fidget out of the corner of her eyes, as if begging her to rip the package open. She chuckled. "Darling, you know half the fun is opening this and watching you squirm."

"Yeah, well, I want you to see it. Come on, already!"

Petra exposed the red velvet box and recognized the logo. She raised an eyebrow and looked at him. She kissed him soundly, then said, "That's for being way too generous, my husband. If I recall correctly, it is the same store where you purchased my amethyst wedding ring. Now I'm excited."

Opening the box, she found a lovely necklace with golden images of a man and woman holding hands. Between them, a smaller figure represented their son. Tears filled her eyes as she examined the symbols of their family. Lifting each of the characters, she found their names engraved. She handed the item to Jacob.

"Please, put it on me."

He complied but asked, "Why are you so teary-eyed? Is it that bad? I thought it a beautiful reminder of what we have as a family."

Petra nodded as the tears escaped her eyes and trailed down her cheek. Her weak smile indicated her agreement, but her tears continued.

Bewildered, Jacob pulled her into his arms. "If you don't like it, I'll get something else. It's all right, I promise."

Petra shook her head and smiled up at him with tears building anew. "No, it's mine, and I think it is gorgeous. Now, it is time for your present."

Reaching into her robe pocket, she removed a wrapped package. Jacob freed his hands to tear open the box. He stared at the plastic container inside, more confused than ever. Then he turned it over and saw the infamous pair of pink lines.

The astonishment was priceless as he babbled, "Really? Ours!! No, kidding?"

Petra beamed. "Yes, and likely close to four months along. Jules reminded me to check my calendar. We've been so busy, and …, I hate forgetting things. EZ tested positive. I tested, and I am, too."

Jacob hugged her fiercely. "So then, why were you crying at my gift?"

Petra touched the lovely necklace and looked at him with love. "Because you'll need to have another figure added soon."

"Yes, honey." He kissed her again. "Happy family. Thank you, sweetheart, for being a part of our amazing gift."

About the Authors

Burkey – Works as a business architect who builds solutions for customers on a good technology foundation. She has written many technology papers, white papers, but finds the freedom of writing fiction a lot more fun. As a child, she helped to lead the kids with exciting new adventures built on make believe characters, was a Girl Scout until high school, and contributed to the community as a young member of a Head Start program. Rox enjoys family, learning, listening to people, travel, outdoor activities, sewing, cooking, and thinking about how to diversify the series.

Breakfield – Works for a high-tech manufacturer as a solution architect, functioning in hybrid data/telecom environments. He considers himself a long-time technology geek, who also enjoys writing, studying World War II history, travel, and cultural exchanges. Charles' love of wine tastings, cooking, and Harley riding has found ways into the stories. As a child, he moved often because of his father's military career, which helps him with the various character perspectives he helps bring to life in the series. He continues to try to teach Burkey humor.

Breakfield and Burkey – started writing non-fictional papers and books, but it wasn't nearly as fun as writing fictional stories. They found it interesting to use the aspects of technology that people are incorporating into their daily lives more and more as a perfect way to create a good guy/bad guy story with elements of travel to the various places they have visited either professionally and personally, humor, romance, intrigue, suspense, and a spirited way to remember people who have crossed paths with them. They love to talk about their stories with private and public book readings. Burkey also conducts regular interviews for Texas authors, which she finds very interesting. Her first interview was, wait for it, Breakfield. You can often find them at local book fairs or other family-oriented events.

The primary series is based on a family organization called R-Group. Recently they have spawned a subgroup that contains some of the original characters as the Cyber Assassins Technology Services (CATS) team. The authors have ideas for continuing the series in both of these tracks. They track the more than 150 characters on a spreadsheet, with a hidden avenue for the future coined The Enigma Chronicles tagged in some portions of the stories. Fan reviews seem to frequently suggest that these would make good television or movie stories, so the possibilities appear endless, just like their ideas for new stories.

They have book video trailers for each of the stories, which can be viewed on YouTube, Amazon's Authors page, or on their website, *www.EnigmaBookSeries.com.* Their website is routinely updated with new interviews, answers to readers' questions, book trailers, and contests. You may also find it fascinating to check out the fun acronyms they create for the stories summarized on their website. Reach out to them at *Authors@EnigmaSeries.com, Twitter@EnigmaSeries,* or *Facebook@TheEnigmaSeries.*

Please provide a fair and honest review on amazon and any other places you post reviews. We appreciate the feedback.

MAGNOLIA BLUFF CRIME CHRONICLES

DEATH WEARS A CRIMSON HAT

MAGNOLIA BLUFF CRIME CHRONICLES

CW HAWES

EULOGY IN BLACK AND WHITE

MAGNOLIA BLUFF CRIME CHRONICLES

CALEB PIRTLE III

THE GREAT PEANUT BUTTER CONSPIRACY

CINDY DAVIS

YOU WON'T KNOW HOW ...OR WHEN

MAGNOLIA BLUFF CRIME CHRONICLES

JAMES R. CALLAN

THE UNDERGROUND AUTHORS PRESENT

THE FLOWER ENIGMA

MAGNOLIA BLUFF CRIME CHRONICLES

BREAKFIELD AND BURKEY

THE SHINE FROM A GIRL IN THE LAKE

MAGNOLIA BLUFF CRIME CHRONICLES

RICHARD SCHWINDT

DEWEY DECIMAL DILEMMA

BOOK 7 MAGNOLIA BLUFF CRIME CHRONICLES

LINDA PIRTLE

JUSTICE

MAGNOLIA BLUFF CRIME CHRONICLES

KELLY MARSHALL

BORN AND BRED TEXAN

MAGNOLIA BLUFF CRIME CHRONICLES

JINX SCHWARTZ

MAGNOLIA BLUFF CRIME CHRONICLES

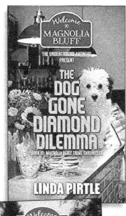

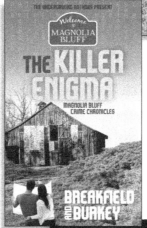

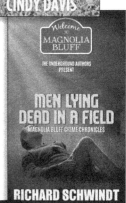

Other stories by Breakfield and Burkey in
The Enigma Series are at *www.EnigmaBookSeries.com*

Other stories by Breakfield and Burkey in
the Heirs Series are at *www.EnigmaBookSeries.com*

We would greatly appreciate
if you would take a few minutes
and provide a review of this work
on Amazon, Goodreads
and any of your other favorite places.

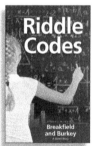

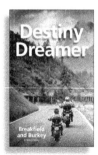

Printed in the USA
CPSIA information can be obtained
at www.ICGtesting.com
LVHW040801011024
792542LV00004B/504